Garden Isle Twins

Garden Isle Twins

Mountains and Valleys and High Tides, Low Tides

Linda Blum

ReadersMagnet, LLC

Garden Isle Twins
Copyright © 2020 by Linda Blum

Published in the United States of America
ISBN Paperback: 978-1-952896-72-9
ISBN eBook: 978-1-952896-73-6

All rights reserved. No part of this publication may be reproduced, stored in a retrieval system or transmitted in any way by any means, electronic, mechanical, photocopy, recording or otherwise without the prior permission of the author except as provided by USA copyright law.

Biblical references are from The King James Version and The Living Bible Paraphrased.

The opinions expressed by the author are not necessarily those of ReadersMagnet, LLC.

ReadersMagnet, LLC
10620 Treena Street, Suite 230 | San Diego, California, 92131 USA
1.619.354.2643 | www.readersmagnet.com

Book design copyright © 2020 by ReadersMagnet, LLC. All rights reserved.
Cover design by Ericka Obando
Interior design by Shemaryl Tampus

Dedication

THIS BOOK IS DEDICATED TO **the many men and women in my family who have left me a legacy by their examples of grace, faith, and love.**

Glossary Of Maine Lingo

APIECE–a ways (Down the road apiece)

AYUH–Used at the end of a sentence or alone to express likes, boredom or sarcasm

BUBBLER–Drinking fountain

CAH–automobile

CARRIAGE–Shopping cart

CHOWDAH–Chowder

CON–corn

COUT–Watch out, warning

CRITTTAH–Animal

CUNNIN–Cute

DOORYAHD–Outside entrance door

DOWN CELLAH–Basement

ELASTIC–rubber band

FRAPPE–Super thick milkshake

GAWMMY–Clumsy

GEEZER–Elderly man

HARD TELLIN–Stumped

HONKIN–Huge

HUMDINGAH–Extraordinary, awesome

MOXIE–Stamina, independence, guts, also a soda that originated in Maine

NOPE–No

NUMB–Stupid action

OUTA STATE/OUTA STATAH–another state/someone of another state

PAHK–Park

PRAYAH HANDLES–Knees

PUCKAH BRUSH–Vegetation that scratches legs

RIGHT OUT STRAIGHT–Very busy

SCRID–Tiny piece

STEAMERS–Clams

TONIC–Soda pop

WICKED–Very

YEP–Yes

YESSAH–Agreement

Contents

Dedication 5
Glossary Of Maine Lingo 7

Mountains And Valleys 11

   Prologue 13
   Chapter One 19
   Chapter Two 27
   Chapter Three 31
   Chapter Four 36
   Chapter Five 43
   Chapter Six 46
   Chapter Seven 51
   Chapter Eight 55
   Chapter Nine 61
   Chapter Ten 64
   Chapter Eleven 68
   Chapter Twelve 71
   Chapter Thirteen 75
   Chapter Fourteen 78
   Chapter Fifteen 83
   Chapter Sixteen 88
   Chapter Seventeen 92
   Chapter Eighteen 94

High Tides, Low Tides **101**
    Chapter One 103
    Chapter Two 108
    Chapter Three 110
    Chapter Four 113
    Chapter Five 116
    Chapter Six 119
    Chapter Seven 122
    Chapter Eight 126
    Chapter Nine 129
    Chapter Ten 131
    Chapter Eleven 133
    Chapter Twelve 135
    Chapter Thirteen 139
    Chapter Fourteen 143
    Chapter Fifteen 146
    Chapter Sixteen 149
    Chapter Seventeen 152
    Chapter Eighteen 155
    Chapter Nineteen 158
    Chapter Twenty 161

Epilogue 167
Note From The Author 175

Mountains And Valleys

Prologue

June 1973

"GET OFF ME!" I HEARD my own voice scream! I was being attacked by a shark! I stilled my arms that were flailing around and took a few deep breaths.

Then, I gently touched the lump on the other air mattress, my fraternal twin sister. According to her ladylike breathing, she was sleeping as if our lives were not going to change in the morning. *She might be able to sleep, but not me!*

My father, Rev. Nathan Miller, is moving us from a city church in Columbus, Ohio to a small church on Garden Isle, Maine, an island which can only be reached by a ferry. I can't believe that I will be living in the middle of the ocean.

My mother is Cynthia Miller, who makes sure every one of her hairs is in place since 5:00 am every day. She has a degree in social work and puts that knowledge to very good use helping all bedraggled people who might come her way. Although she won't be working for the Columbus Social Service Center anymore, I have a feeling she'll find plenty of people to hold up until they can lift themselves up by their own bootstraps.

The moving van rolled out of our driveway the day before yesterday. Dad left for Garden Isle in our black Beetle two weeks ago, while the three of us are leaving in the Chevy station wagon at the crack of dawn. The trip will take about twenty hours as we pass through several states.

Doesn't this all sound exciting?

I'm the adventurous type, but I don't want to go live on an island away from Tony. He and I are both fifteen, and we are sure we're in love. Last evening we met at Jack's Soda Shoppe secretly. (Our relationship was always a secret, even from my twin.) While we ate burgers and sipped cokes, Tony whispered, "I can't say goodbye, Jeanne." I took a close look at Tony as if to memorize his face. His brown hair flopped onto his broad forehead and his lips quivered. Hazel eyes met brown eyes as we clung to each other. In unison, we whispered, "Write me." Before we split up, Tony hung a heart-shaped locket around my neck. I tucked it inside my blouse.

Later, I let myself into the house. I was so trying not to act guilty. UH OH! My mother was on the other side of the door. "Honey, I know you needed to see your best friend, but if you had come home sooner you could have helped Ruby and me clean the parsonage and pack up the car. We got most of it done regardless." *PHEWW!*

Putting her arm around me, Mom led me into the bare living room where Ruby sat on the carpet. My twin rolled her eyes. *I can't really blame her when I wasn't here to help.* I came and hugged her. "Ruby, I'm sorry."

"It's ok I guess."

Like a drill sergeant entering barracks Mom marched into the room carrying her to-do list. "Jeanne Ruth and Ruby Jane, we've got some things to go over, so listen up."

"First, I want to encourage you to get plenty of sleep for our long trip tomorrow. We'll all get up at 5:00. The car will need to be loaded with your air mattresses and overnight bags, and we'll stop at the Corner Diner for breakfast. Today we'll go as far as Philadelphia, about a ten-hour trip. I've already made reservations at Howard Johnson's Motor Inn. We'll need to arise at 4:00 to be ready to start out at 5:00. That will get us to Covington in time to catch the last scheduled ferry crossing. This rapid-fire speech made Mama a little breathless. She looked at me, "Jeanne, could you please get me a drink of water? We left out three glasses on the counter." She croaked, "Thanks."

Out in the kitchen, the wall phone was ringing, and I rushed to answer it. "Hello."

Laughter erupted on the other end, "Is this my Jeanne or my Ruby?"

"Jeanne, Daddy."

"You're going to love it here! Ayuh." Nathan chuckled, "This place is like another world,"

I just bet it is. "I can't wait to see you day after tomorrow, Daddy. I've missed you."

"I've missed you too. I love my girls. I've been trying to settle our new home some since the moving van arrived yesterday. There's a lot to do still, but I know we'll all work together as usual. I have to run. Hug your mother and sister for me. Goodbye, Honey-girl. Be safe and have fun. Ayuh."

"Dad, what's Ayuh?"

"It's used in many different ways here. This time I meant "Yes, I pray so". It's one of many words you'll be learning; some are really funny."

"Ok, Dad. I love you. Bye." I heard coughing. *I almost forgot Mom's water!*

I fetched the water glass and filled it. When I handed her the water, I kissed my mother and sister good night. Ruby and I crept up the stairs, crawled into our sleeping bags, and drifted off to sleep. But I was restless.

* * *

After the nightmare, I stretched out in the semi-darkness and thoughts went whirling through my overtired brain. To tell you the truth, I was afraid to go back to sleep.

Even though Dad's been trained for this move, it won't be easy for him. He's used to sitting on the platform wearing vestments. Everything will be so different. Guitars and drums and modern songs… People, including us, dressed casually for church…. But Mama will be dressed up; I guarantee that. (Smile) It'll be nice for us all to sit together on the front row. Wow! We'll be in the "Jesus Freak Movement!"

Ruby stirred and turned toward me. "I'm nervous, Jeanne. We're leaving our whole life behind. You know how hard it is for me to make new friends." She whimpered softly.

"Our family will be together, and we'll help each other face all those strangers in that strange place. Dad said Maine is actually like another world."

Always studious, Ruby said, "I have been reading as much as I could about it, and it does sound like a strange place…" *She has fallen back asleep but not me!*

At 5:00 I looked out from what used to be our bedroom window at the gorgeous sunrise. I wanted to jump out of bed and fetch my camera to take snapshots of the reds and blues swishing together as if by a giant paint brush. *What a gorgeous sunrise!*

"Girls, we need to leave within the hour." The car was packed with cherished breakables, but two frames still hung on the living room wall. "Jeanne and Ruby, could you please put your bags in the car. Then, put the framed items on top of everything. Make sure you secure it all." Ruby took down the portrait of our family, leaving me to remove the other frame. Before wrapping it tightly in newspaper, I read the words again from "House by the Side of the Road:"

> Let me live in my house by the side of the road
> And be a friend to man.
> I know there are brook-gladdened meadows ahead
> And mountains of wearisome height.
> That the road passes on through the long afternoon
> And stretches away to the night.
>
> But still I rejoice when the travelers rejoice
> And weep with the strangers that moan.

From a poem by Sam Walter Foss (1858-1911)

I couldn't help thinking about the long list of men, women, and children who had lived with us for brief to lengthy periods over the years. *How many will come to our new place? How many faces of loss and desperation will come to our door?*

"It's time to leave, girls!" I took one last look at my life-long home as it faded from view.

Chapter One

"*A*RE WE IN MAINE YET?" Sleepily, Jeanne queried her mother from the passenger seat barely holding onto the Road Atlas. *No surprise since I was fidgety all night...*

"No, but we have only two hundred miles or so left," answered her mother glancing over her shoulder.

Jeanne turned toward Ruby, who was jammed in beside the boxes of precious china. Her sister balanced a book about Maine on her lap. "There are lots of birds near the seashore like the puffins that live only in Maine. We can go birdwatching together, Jeanne."

Cynthia interrupted, "Girls, the ferry won't be covered, so we will no doubt get wind–blown, and we may get saltwater–sprayed a bit. I'll cover my hair with this kerchief. You may want to secure your hair."

Jeanne had curly, thick reddish-brown totally unmanageable hair that fell to her mid-back and was held on both sides with barrettes. On the other hand, Ruby's hair was shiny golden blonde which she normally wore in a sleek shoulder-length pageboy. Ruby secured a ponytail, and Jeanne fashioned one loose braid.

Finally, they saw the sign for Covington, Maine. Jeanne beat her chest a couple of times. "Me and this trusty 'ole Road Atlas did it!" *But where is that ferry?*

As the Chevy circled around the rock wall barrier, Ruby shouted. "Mom, stop!"

"Why? Wh-a-at? Cynthia rolled to a stop at a nearby pull-off.

Shouts rang out as the twins raced over to their grinning father.

Cynthia checked her appearance in the rearview mirror; then, she walked gingerly over to where her husband stood. "I thought we'd be meeting you on Garden Isle…"

Nathan puffed out his cheeks. "I decided to surprise you and take the ferry ride with my girls. I already paid the fares. I'll hop in and drive you there. Jeanne, can you squeeze in beside Ruby? It isn't far, just down the road apiece."

Jeanne grinned at the colloquialism. "Sure, I will, Dad. I'll pile the boxes up to make some room. Ruby, please move over!"

"SQUEE-eee! Wawk-Wawk-Wawk! SQUEE-eee! Wawk-Wawk-Wawk!" Cynthia squeaked and covered her ears, "What was that?"

"Those, m' ladies, are seagulls. You'll be hearing that melodious bird from morning until night. I promise you'll get used to their squawking. Here's the ferry, right on schedule." "Let's bring this 'ole bucket of bolts into line." Nate had slowed the Chevy to a crawl.

"All these cars and trucks will fit on there?" Ruby pointed.

"Just you wait and see. We'll slip in right here." With that said, Nathan entered the line of vehicles waiting to board.

After driving onto the ferry, the family climbed out and went to sit on one of the broadside benches A ferry operator and his first mate scurried about buttoning down the hatches and securing everything for setting sail. The first mate, who looked close to their age, ducked under the door that separated the cars from the passenger area. His strawberry blonde hair stuck out like wings from the sides of his seaman's cap. His blueberry eyes darted around checking that all was in order.

Nathan led his family to a bench. As they gazed at the sea, they could barely tell where there was a horizon. Several cormorants flew over chirping softly.

The mother and her girls all wore dresses. Cynthia sat demurely crossing her ankles, her sweater flung over her shoulders. Jeanne leaned forward and crossed her legs. Ruby sat up straight with her hands folded, feet crossed, and eyes lowered toward the deck. The twins pulled on their sweaters. The cool, damp air, mixed with the sprays of salty water, brought an uncomfortable chill.

Plump, red-faced Pastor Nate, so named by the Island folks, plunked down beside his wife; he threw his arm over her shoulders and brushed her cool cheek with his plump lips. He didn't look much like a minister in his plaid shirt and jeans and sporting a beard.

"Jeanne, the skirt…" Her mother whispered through tight lips. Jeanne gave her skirt a little tug. *I'd like to wear a mini-skirt like other girls do who aren't pastors' daughters.*

"I know you've never been to Maine or to the ocean, so this move is destined to prove to be an adventure! I could tell you about Garden Isle now while we're sailing, but I thought you'd like to experience everything firsthand. Then, Nathan began to chuckle. *Just you wait, my girls.*

"Uh Oh, Ruby, you look a little …white." Jeanne touched her twin's arm.

"I think the first mate just winked at me." Ruby trembling, whispered in Jeanne's ear.

"Can you hold on a little while? We're almost home." Her father urged.

Cynthia yawned. "Where you lead, I follow, my dear husband."

The ferry crawled to a stop. The family rose. Jeanne's hazel eyes looked up at Ruby's pale blue ones, and then she lightly patted her twin, a statue stuck onto the deck. "Come on, Ruby."

Ruby and her father towered over Jeanne and her mother as they strolled over to the car.

* * *

A hilly fishing village of colorful buildings, as if they were piled one on the other, spread out in front of the bow. On either side of the dock ramp were trawlers, cabin cruisers, yachts, commercial fishing boats, schooners, sailboats, and sloops. Jeanne was awestruck at all the seaside sights. A weathered signpost read: WELCOME TO GARDEN ISLE, Pop. 3,264.

A fisherman with a wrinkled face and snowy white hair, beard, and mustache was bringing a boat laden with fish to shore. Pulling out some thick rope, he looked up to see gulls wheeling above the boat. One swooped down to nab a fish from his catch. The old man whisked off his bright yellow floppy hat and waved it. "Shoo! Shoo!"

The heather and purple heart flowers were blooming along the further side of the rickety boardwalk. Jeanne smacked her gum and bounced from one foot to the other. Ruby held her book looking up details about the birds and blooms she was trying to identify.

On his way to direct drivers to start their vehicles, the first mate came up to their car leaning on the open window. "Hi, Pastor Nate, I'd like to meet your family."

After introductions, Patrick walked straight over to Ruby's side window. Her chin touched her chest. "Hi. I bet you'll like Garden Isle." He glanced at the books she held. Ruby looked up and met his gaze. "It's nice to meet you, Ruby. Jeanne, Ma'am." Whistling, the handsome boy strode back to instruct the driver behind them.

Slowly Nate drove off from the ferry and bumped onto the ramp that connected to the narrow street near the waterfront. He stopped in front of the Harbor Café. "I made reservations here for the seafood buffet, all-you-can-eat." Nathan patted his ample paunch. "Come on, let's go in." He opened the door and walked in behind the ladies.

The buffet consisted of fried haddock, lobster tails, clams, and oysters on the half shell. The salad bar stretched across the restaurant for twenty feet. After eating until they were stuffed, the family got back into their car.

The sunset of pink, purple, and orange hues reflected upon the ocean water. Flocks of sandpipers skittered across the shore scavenging for morsels. Gulls dove into the sparkling water nabbing fish. The cool damp air smelled salt–fishy.

"The next stop is our new home; it's a humdinger if you ask me." Completing a short drive uphill, Nathan stopped in a circular driveway facing a large, old-looking sea captain's house. Before anyone exited the car, Nathan explained that it had been donated to the church for a parsonage. The outside of the house was white with a green roof and trim including shutters. The lawn was overgrown with patches of lupine. "I didn't have time to get everything done," he shrugged.

"We'll help with the gardening and maybe procure some assistance from church folks." *Mom is planning it all now* Cynthia looked around and jotted down some landscaping ideas.

Adorned with an ornate brass knocker and a mercury glass doorknob, the wooden front door was massive. A rectangular frieze of a whale surrounded by sculpted waves shone silvery over the door, and to the left of the porch stairs, a brass flagpole glistened while the faded flag blew in the gentle breeze. The family tromped up the wide rock stairs and crossed the porch.

Nathan turned the key, and flung the door open with a flourish. "Da! Da!!" They stepped directly into a living room resplendent with knotty pine wainscoting and a marble fireplace. Elaborate molding surrounded the bare windows, and the elegant tin tiled ceiling reached to about ten feet. Cynthia's mouth flew open as if she were a frog about to catch a fly. The twins grabbed each other jumping up and down on the wide-board floor.

Their furniture and piles of marked boxes had been brought into the appropriate rooms. The family set off to view the rest of the house. Their first stop, the kitchen that was too large to be cozy. However, it was well-equipped with a wood cook stove that had a shelf for setting bread to rise, a Frigidaire refrigerator, a row of painted cupboards, a long sideboard, and a black soapstone sink with brass faucets. A formal dining room adjoined the kitchen. "We'll need to get some furniture for this room. It could be quite elegant." Cynthia smiled and wrote that need on her pad then stuck the pencil behind her ear.

Next, Nathan led them to the stairs ascending from the hall which led to the back door. "There are five rooms up there and a bathroom," Nathan pointed. At the head of the stairs they found that the bathroom contained a large claw foot tub and a toilet that flushed by the pull of a brass chain.

"Jeanne Ruth Miller and Ruby Jane Miller, you will each have your own bedroom. Pick out the ones you want." Nathan grinned as he crossed his arms.

The girls chose adjacent rooms. Jeanne's room was twice the size of the one she'd shared with Ruby in Ohio. The bedroom would later be spruced up with fresh wallpaper and curtains. *My very own room…cool…* Jeanne flopped onto her bare mattress and promptly went to sleep.

When she awakened in the darkened room, she crossed over to the window, sat on the window seat, and peered out. Dancing her right leg, Jeanne thought about her life as a preacher's kid. *People ask my advice and counsel when my parents aren't around. I'm not a social worker… that's Mama. They ask me theological questions…I'm not the preacher…that's Daddy. They all expect me to fill in when someone's absent. My life is not my own. My life is always about the church, but when I turn eighteen…*

"Come see my new room. There are shelves for the porcelain dolls I made!"

"See what's in my room." Jeanne waved her hand in a circle. "I have shelves too where I can display all my model cars and ships." The twins held hands as they walked out of Jeanne's room.

Chapter Two

JEANNE WAS STARTLED FROM SLEEP. *Bring! Bring! Mom's alarm, 5:00…*More sounds…men shouting, foghorns blaring, gulls squawking… *That bird is so annoying.*

She pried her eyes open. A bright light was flashing through her window every few seconds. *Cover my head… Oh boy, it's no use.* She struggled to sit up in the semi-darkness, and managed to get her bare feet onto the cold wooden floor. Then, she readied herself for the day's adventures.

The twins entered the kitchen at the same time. "The top of the day to you, lassies." Nathan bowed his head. "Father, I pray for your blessing and guidance this day. Thank you for my beautiful girls who are here to share it with me. Bless this first meal in our new home." In Jesus' name I pray. Amen."

"We have a busy day ahead of us." Cynthia examined her to-do list closely. "That includes going to the general store and the church. This dry cereal and juice will be enough until we eat lunch out. We're grocery shopping; I'll cook a nice breakfast tomorrow."

Pushing his chair back, Nathan stood. "Let's go. Time's a wastin'. First stop, the Garden Isle General Store."

* * *

The weathered boardwalk and wharf looked silvery in the sunlight. To the east was a stately red and white lighthouse with a connected house; two small buildings sat off to one side. A long, narrow wooden walkway with railings on both sides had been built over rocks that jutted out from the island about thirty yards.

A pungent smell of fish filled the air. They all trudged up four steps to the general store's entrance; over their heads protruded a patched blue and white striped awning. Ruby stopped to read the "Help Wanted" sign taped to the window.

The Garden Isle General Store's interior was larger than it looked from the outside. They saw a deli counter where a large jar of pickled eggs and varieties of penny candy had been assembled. Three unmatched tables were pushed together and upholstered red chairs patched with duct tape held a gaggle of geezers.

"'Lo, Rev'rund Millah!" shouted a burly man whose grey hair was flat when he whisked off his hat. "Introduce us to your perty gals. Name's Raymond Taylor, Ma'am, girls."

Following the introductions, Nathan asked, "What can you tell us about clamming?"

A skinny, red-haired, pock-faced man named Owen answered, "Clam flats are off that away, go apiece and bang a left. I'll have you know you can get what you need for clammin' right in he-ah, ayuh. You and yo' gals will need some clam diggah pants and rubbah boots. Ask Chahlee ovah theyah what equipment you'll need. He's the boss. Low tide's at 2 o'clock sharp t'day. Bangor Daily News reports tides." Owen held up the coffee-stained paper.

Cynthia inquired, "Can we go down to the wharf to buy lobsters and crabs directly from the fishermen?"

"Yessah, Ma'am, but Jake's Fish Market is just 'round the connah. He buys 'n sells it all fresh." replied Raymond as his gnarled hands braced the back of his thick neck.

Ruby hurried to apply for a job in the store. Jeanne went to find the clam digger pants and boots. Nathan and Cynthia went to the back to see Charlie and bought a clam roller and two clam hoes. They purchased enough groceries for the week.

"I got the job. I'll start training Monday!" Ruby was excited.

Jeanne hugged her twin while their parents smiled.

After loading all the purchases into the back of the station wagon, the Millers drove to the A & W drive-in stand. Jeanne spotted a carhop balancing an order on a metal tray. "I'd love to do this!" *The uniform is so cool.*

The carhop rollerskated over to the car wearing a brown vest over a white short-sleeved blouse, an orange a-line skirt that fell just above the knees, a white apron, and a brown triangular hat with a white and orange-striped band. "My name's Laurie. I'll be your waitress.

"Does a carhop have to use roller skates?" Jeanne asked barely controlling her excitement.

"No… You don't really have to. Just have to hop from one car to the other." (Giggle)

"Are they hiring?"

"I heard they'll need someone in a couple of weeks to cover for vacations." Holding her pencil over her order pad the waitress stood still, "What will you folks have today?"

Nathan grinned, "Four Papa burgers, four large French fries, four apple turnovers, and four root beers." He turned to Cynthia. "I thought I'd just go ahead and order for all of us."

"Papa burgers?" Cynthia's brow wrinkled.

"They have those and Mama burgers, Teen burgers, and Baby burgers. The root beer is frothy and cold because the mugs are kept in the freezer. The ice cream comes in cones, frappes, and root beer floats." Nathan plunked his hands on the steering wheel in satisfaction as if he'd just recited the Declaration of Independence.

First, the carhop brought out A&W root beer securing the tray to the bottom of the driver's side window. Next, the Papa burgers and orders of fries were brought out and last the turnovers.

After the family had eaten, Nathan blew the horn once. Flashing the headlights was the usual signal, but the sun was strong. Jeanne hopped out, ran inside and saw the manager.

Climbing back into the Chevy, Jeanne jabbered a mile-a-minute. "I can start in two weeks. I'll come in to train the week before that Wednesday. They're giving me three of those cute uniforms. My pay will be good too…"

"That's my girl." Nathan turned around and smiled.

"Good, Dear. We need to get home and get these groceries put away. After that, we'll go to the church." Cynthia reached back and patted Jeanne's arm.

Chapter Three

SEACREST CHAPEL WAS LOCATED ON the wild flower-strewn southern end of Garden Isle. Ruby was frantically flipping pages of her "Flowers of Maine" book as they drew near to the church. She pointed. "Over there I see tiger and lemon lilies, and next to the church I see a patch of lily of the valley."

"Let's all go in now." Pastor Nate pointed at a freshly painted sign. "The church was formerly the Garden Isle Community Church, but the board agreed to change the name to Seacrest Chapel. It's a fitting name since we're one of the Chapel churches."

After they have climbed the narrow fifteen steps, they stepped through the narrow sanctuary door. Jeanne pointed, "Look! The pulpit looks like the bow of a ship. This is so cool!"

Ruby stared at the high cathedral ceiling. "Oh, there's beautiful wood up there."

"I won't like sitting on those hard wooden benches." Jeanne frowned.

"We'll bring some cushions." Cynthia wrote a reminder on her ever-present pad; then she asked, "Where are the restrooms, Nate?"

Red-faced, her husband sputtered the answer. "We-e-e just ha-a-ve two outhouses out that way." His finger trembled toward the window. "This fall we plan to install a couple of chemical toilets since there is no plumbing in here. I guess we'll have to make do until then."

"It's a little chilly. Saturday evening I'll build a fire." Nathan pointed at the pot-bellied stove. "There's another stove downstairs that heats the Sunday School rooms."

A buxom woman peered around the corner. She wore braids twisted around her head, and she wiped her pudgy hands on a soiled apron stretched over a faded blue house dress. "'Lo, Pastor Nate," Holding the broom like a drawn sword, she skidded in front of the family inspecting each one closely. Tugging Nathan's beard, she blurted, "Shave off that thing!" Eyeing the hem of Jeanne's skirt, she looked at Cynthia, "A pastor's daughter ought to cover her knees. It looks like you could lower that hem quite a bit!" She smiled warmly at Ruby, "You seem like an upstanding young lady."

Jeanne had heard enough. Shaking, she made a beeline for the door, ran down the stairs, and raced out to the car. Bang! She threw herself onto the backseat. An\gry, burning tears threatened to spill down her cheeks. *Ruby's a perfect pastor's daughter. I want to be like normal people. Whatever that witch's name is should keep her trap shut...*

The other door opened, and Ruby slid inside. "Jeanne..."

Arms folded tightly and lips pressed together, her twin whispered dangerously, "Get out."

"Arf! Arf!" Jeanne and Ruby looked out the window trying to spot a barking dog. There on the shoreline a shiny black body flopped onto the sand, flippers dancing.

"It's a seal!" Car doors slammed. Feet raced to the seashore. Sisters stood arm-in-arm mesmerized by the harbor seal's antics. Ruby faced her twin. "Come on, Jeanne. We can go back in now. That woman just drove away."

"Oh, okay. Who is she anyhow?"

"Her name's Violet Moore."

"I hope I don't see that loudmouth again but fat chance of that."

The girls came through the sanctuary door to find another woman whose strawberry blonde hair peeked out from under the cotton kerchief she'd tied in the back.

Showing her perfect teeth, she smiled at the girls, "You must be Jean and…"

Jeanne interrupted, "Gee-nee."

"Well, Jeanne and Ruby, we're all so overjoyed your family came to us. I'm Maisie O'Connor. By the way, I have a son about your age. My Patrick has a summer job as first mate on the ferry. When your parents come back inside, I have a …well, here they are now."

"We've all been planning a clam bake welcome party for Saturday at 6:00. It'll be held behind Jake's store," Maisie announced eagerly.

Grinning, Pastor Nate accepted the invitation. "That sounds wicked good, Mrs. O'Connor. We'd be honored. Thanks. We're going clamming Friday and will bring some with us."

* * *

Later that day, the family was ready to pray a blessing over supper when they heard a sound coming from down cellar. Nathan opened the door and hollered, "Whoever you are come up and have some supper."

Shuffling feet trudged up the wooden stairs. A boy emerged. His voice cracked. "Thanks. I'm hungry."

"Right this way," replied Nathan. He guided the boy to the kitchen.

He looks to be around eleven or twelve. Jeanne and Ruby smiled while Cynthia indicated where he could sit and went to the cupboard to get another place setting.

Without uttering another word, their unexpected guest finished his meal in record time. Stifled gasps were heard around the table when he finally lifted his head. His left cheek was black and blue, his left eye was half-closed, and the left side of his nose was covered in dried blood. Dark curly hair, brown eyes, and full lips on the right side revealed a good looking boy.

Nathan introduced his family to their guest.

Cynthia went over to the boy, who obviously needed her gentle care and assurance. Drawing a deep breath, she spoke slowly at eye-level, "We're glad you're here and want to help you. Would you tell us a little bit about yourself?"

His ears were turning red, and he blurted, "I'm Sebastian, and I'm twelve. My Daddy is a boat builder. I was painting a boat but weren't quick 'bout it. He had had a few, and I got this." Tears sprang to his eyes.

"How'd you end up in our basement, Son?" inquired Nathan as he reached out and touched Sebastian's skinny arm.

"I came in through the bulkhead. Am I in trouble?" Sebastian lifted his shoulders and let them drop.

"No. Where do you live? Can we drive you home?" Nathan offered.

"I don't want to go home now, but my Granny will let me come to her house for a while."

"I'll grab my keys, and we'll drive you there now."

"Can you wait a minute?" Jeanne ran up the stairs to her room and promptly came back down. Walking over to Sebastian, she handed him a shiny model Cadillac. "I want you to have this before you leave with Mama and Daddy. I made it myself."

"Thanks, Jeanne." He mumbled his appreciation when he reached for it.

"Can you show us how to get to your grandmother's house?" Nathan asked.

"Yessah." Sebastian followed Nathan and Cynthia to the Beetle.

When the house was empty, Jeanne's spirit brightened. "What do you say we walk down to the beach? We can leave a note that we'll get back before dark."

"I don't know…"

"Oh come on. It'll be fun. We'll see birds and flowers. Bring your books."

"OK, but we'll need to dress warm." The girls pulled on slacks, sweaters, and jackets.

Then they quickly wrote a note and shut the back door.

Chapter Four

Sounds of people singing drew the twins toward a cove shielded by a myrtle hedge. People were sitting on blankets, and two guys were standing over by the life guard station, one with a crewcut and short, athletic body holding a Bible and one with strawberry blonde hair strumming a guitar. Ruby stopped. "Isn't that the boy from the ferry?"

"Maybe that's him."

Feet sinking into the sand, the twins came through a path lined with reeds. They made their way to the snapping bonfire. The beachfront was crowded with young people. Two smiling girls wearing colorful bell bottoms beckoned them; the one with French braids patted the plaid blanket whispering, "Sit here with us." Jeanne and Ruby sat and joined in the singing.

> "Are you tired of chasing pretty rainbows?
> Are you tired of spinning round and round?
> Wrap up all the shattered dreams of your life.
> And at the feet of Jesus lay them down.
> Give them all. Give them all. Give them all to Jesus,
> Shattered dreams, wounded hearts, broken toys,
> Give them all. Give them all. Give them all to Jesus,
> And He will turn your sorrow into joy…"

"Evie Tornquist wrote *Give Them All.* When you look in your mirror first thing in the morning, do you see anything you'd like to see changed? Maybe that hair sticking straight up in all directions, or those rumpled p.j.s. (giggles) During this coming week let's all take a good look at our lives. You can never be so bad that our Savior's love can't reach you. No matter how good you are, He won't love you any more than He does right now. Jesus loves every one of us the same. My name's Brian Smith; I'm the youth leader at Seacrest Chapel." Brian gestured toward the guitarist, "Let's thank Patrick O' Connor for leading the music. (clapping)

Welcome everyone, to our seaside singalong. Now put on your listening ears. After we've gathered and had a short devotion at Creation House tomorrow morning at 8:00, we'll begin this summer's free surfing lessons. If you want to learn to surf, you'll need to register inside Creation House and sign out a surfboard and wetsuit. If you're under eighteen, bring a permission note from your parents. Lessons are available for those sixteen and over. The House is open for rapping and hanging out until 6:00 p.m. Monday through Friday. My wife, Julia, and I will always be around and will have drinks and snacks available. Pastor Nate will be popping in from time to time too."

Following the announcements, the beach crowd sang three songs by Andrae Crouch. Acapella, *Through it All* brought forth some sounds of sniffles. Jeanne talked with the kids sitting around them while her shy sister nodded and said, "Um hum" periodically.

"Tomorrow night, only if you want to, bring a private note of some things you feel you want to give over to Jesus, We'll burn them all in the bonfire. Good night. Go with God."

"We'd better hurry home," cautioned Ruby. Rising, they stopped in their tracks when a flock of strange-looking birds waddled across the sand. "Those are those cute puffin birds. Maine is the only place where they live. They can carry several fish in their beaks at once."

Beginning their brisk walk back home, the twins pulled up their collars. Seabirds were quietly finding places to rest for the night. The red sun sinking slowly behind the horizon splashed every color of the rainbow across the azure sky.

"I think I'd like to learn to surf. Wouldn't you?" Jeanne turned toward Ruby.

"I don't know if I will. There are sharks in the ocean." Ruby shivered, not from exposure to the cool night air.

Pounding feet caused Jeanne to glance in her peripheral vision. A man was quickly gaining ground behind them. The twins began to jog.

"Ruby, I saw you at the beach…" Patrick bent over panting. "I wanted to invite you to go out for ice cream after church next Sunday."

Ruby pondered her answer. "Well, I'll ask Mama and Daddy. Thanks."

* * *

Finding their parents snuggling on the porch swing, the twins sat in matching wicker chairs. Jeanne's brow furrowed. "Is Sebastian okay?"

"Yes girls. He's with his grandmother. She seems sweet and caring." Cynthia smiled.

"We met Brian at the beach bonfire. He said we could learn to surf for free. It'll start tomorrow at 8. I want to do it. Please! I'll be sixteen in two weeks. Can you ask him? Please!" Jeanne pleaded. One foot "beat the drum" on the porch floor.

"I'll call to see what he says." Nathan went inside and called from the wall phone. A few minutes later he came back out nodding.

This is one time I'll be glad to get up early. Jeanne and Ruby retired to their rooms.

Next morning, excited for her new adventures, Jeanne walked briskly and arrived at Creation House a half hour early. "I'm Jeanne Miller. Dad called you last night. Here's the note."

"Yes, you're Pastor Nate's daughter. Welcome. Would you like to read the scripture for the devotion?" *Of course I will. That's the role I play.*

"Sure, Mr. Smith, I can do that. Where's the Bible?" Jeanne forced a smile.

As soon as six others registered and picked up equipment, devotions began. "This is one of Pastor Nate's twins. Jeanne. Everyone make her welcome. Please read Psalm 107:23-31, this time our reading is from the new Living Bible." Jeanne forced a smile, nodded, and read:

23. "And then there are the sailors sailing the seven seas, plying the trade routes of the world. 24. They, too, observe the power of God in action. 25. He calls to the storm winds; the waves rise high. 26. Their ships are tossed to the heavens and sink again to the depths; the sailors cringe in terror. 27. They reel and stagger like drunkards and are at their wit's end. 28. Then they cry to the Lord in their trouble, and he saves them. 29. He calms the storm and stills the waves. 30. What a blessing is that stillness, as he brings them safely into harbor! 31. Oh, that these men would praise the Lord for his lovingkindness and for all of his wonderful deeds!" *I haven't had the chance to consider whether or not I believe this stuff or not. It's my family…It's expected…*

"Thank you, Jeanne." Brian retrieved his Bible. 'Prayer does not fit us for the greater work. Prayer is the greater work' a quote from Oswald Chambers. "Let's pray together. Our Father, we pray that you will guide us as we learn, and please protect us today upon the waves. In Jesus' name we pray, Amen."

"We'll start this surf school in shallow water, where waves are only 5 to 6 feet high. Don't be disappointed; 20 foot waves will come later. When you remove wetsuits please wash them in this tub. Washing and drying instructions are over there on the wall. God bless you all as you learn to surf today. Today the sun and the surf are perfect."

Jeanne donned a wetsuit, grabbed a surfboard, and ran through the sand to join the others for instructions. Brian made certain that his teaching and demonstrating made sense. Then, the first timers practiced. Jeanne fell off the board a few times; but triumphant at last, she stood and rode a wave into shore. She pumped a fist in the air and promptly collapsed onto the sandy beach. She watched the cumulus clouds swerve over the sky.

Knowing her family had some important plans laid out, Jeanne leaped up and walked briskly back to Creation House, showered, changed, and cleaned the wetsuit. When she came out, a flock of cormorants were squealing as they flew low. *They must be congratulating me.*

* * *

As she came in view of the front door, she saw her family stepping off the porch.

"Come on, Jeanne, we're leaving now." Her Dad called. She ran to the VW and hopped in.

Later, the car stopped at a pink stone mansion. Cedar hedges lined both sides over from the front door. "This is where you'll be going to school, one of the first magnet schools in Maine. Locals call it the Fish School. The theme for the upper grades is Marine Biology. We'll go in and register you now. You'll like the principal, Mr. Walker."

The old mansion had been converted into a first through twelfth grade school that could accommodate 130 students. Jeanne and Ruby, numbers 127 and 128, registered into the junior class. Mr. Walker had sparse brown hair that formed a two inch ring from ear to ear and kind hazel eyes peering out of wire rims. He wore a paisley print double-breasted jacket, lilac shirt, and blue bowtie. Resting both elbows on the desk, Mr. Walker turned toward the girls.

"We're proud to be one of the first magnet schools in the state. Most of the students and teachers live on the island, but some come and go by ferry. It doesn't matter what town they're from; anyone nearby can send in an application. Students from the mainland are chosen by picking names from a hat. Our school is hands-on learning, and every subject has a marine theme. High school students will document ecosystems and observe whales and dolphins." He smiled, "Would you like to see your classroom?"

The twins tromped up the long flight of stairs behind Mr. Walker. Off to the right they peered into a well-equipped classroom. Upon entering, the girls walked around the room and glanced at the exhibits and posters of marine life. "Thank you, Mr. Walker. It's so cool!" Jeanne hopped on one foot. Ruby nodded enthusiastically.

Exiting the school, Nathan glanced back and turned to the girls. "Aren't you glad we came here to Garden Isle now?" *Well, the good things are adding up, but I really miss Tony...*

Chapter Five

*T*HIS FEELS WEIRD. JEANNE WAS walking with her family across the long, narrow bridge so they could have a tour of the lighthouse. Nearing the end of the trek across the bridge, Nathan pointed to the slanted ramp that led to a rocky incline. It became steeper as they drew closer to the lighthouse. A rock path brought them to the front of the attached keeper's house.

Breathing heavily and holding their sides, the family struggled up to the door. Violet Moore turned the doorknob and peered out. "Can I help you, Pastor?"

Jeanne turned her back. *My worst nightmare…she's the meanest…*

"We came to take the tour, Mrs. Moore. Will Mr. Moore be showing us around?"

"Useless isn't here right now; he's gone fishing. You can tour the lighthouse. That will be $8.00, $2.00 each." Violet's outstretched hand received the fees. "Thank you."

Violet called over her shoulder, "Lizzy, come here, and take these people to the top." She looked at Nathan, "I'll explain things when you come back down here."

Jeanne turned around to observe the long, sad face of a teenage girl who wore over-sized overalls. Her feet wobbled in her scuffed penny loafers. "Okay, Mother. This way please. There are ninety stairs to the top, but there is a landing halfway up." *Ninety steps!*

After introductions, they all silently climbed the narrow metal stairs to the landing and gazed over the sturdy railing. "You should all get a drink here before we go the rest of the way," cautioned Lizzy. After ten minutes rest, they climbed to the windowed top and went outside to stand at the circular railing.

"This is breathtaking! I can see everything!" Ruby leaned on the wrought iron.

Jeanne stood beside her twin and turned toward Lizzy. "Can you tell me who Useless is, if I may ask?" *That seems mean to call someone that.*

"He's my foster father." Lizzy's expression was pained as she turned away.

Always curious, Jeanne pointed at the two cabins. "Who lives there?"

"Grand Daddy. He's a sea captain and takes me out in the cabin cruiser sometimes. The other cabin is for people we rescue." Remembering her duties, Lizzy added, "Do you have any other questions?"

"How often does the light flash? What are the hours? Do you have electricity? Do you have a phone?" The family peppered Lizzy with questions.

"The light flashes every fifteen seconds from 6 pm to 6 am. We have a generator. No phone. We use a CB radio."

Ruby glanced down at the stringy copper-colored hair, "How old are you?"

"Seventeen years old. How old are you?"

"We're fifteen. We'll have our birthdays in ten days. Maybe you can come to our party." Ruby smiled at Lizzy's upturned face.

"I'd love to if she'll let me."

"Lollygag! What's keeping you? We need to finish the tour within the hour!" Violet hollered up the stairwell.

Donald Moore, still wearing fishy-smelling oil cloth overalls, met the family at the bottom. "Thanks, Lizzy. I'll finish the tour for the pastor." He laid his hand on Lizzy's shoulder. She walked away, and Donald faced the tourists. "Lighthouse livin' is hahd. Wintah's a bear. Durin'some wintah storms we haven't gone shoppin' for food for a month. There's no runnin' watah heah so we bring some ovah two or three times a week, and we make do with a chemical toilet. We turn on the light at dusk and shut it off at dawn every day. In the morning we clean and polish the glass. Curtains are closed during sunny days to prevent fires. Are there questions, folks?"

> "Can Lizzy come to supper and the beach meeting tonight?" Jeanne blurted.
>
> "What do they want, Useless?" Violet called from the kitchen. Donald told her.
>
> "They asked if I could come now." Lizzy informed her foster parents.
>
> "You can go, but mind your Ps and Qs." Violet scowled, "See that she does."
>
> "May I have a minute to change?" Lizzy looked at Cynthia.
>
> "My Dear, I'm sure the girls can find something for you to wear."
>
> Lizzy smiled and happy tears sprang to her eyes while the twins nodded enthusiastically.

Chapter Six

"You're just a little shorter than I am, Lizzy. Why don't you pick out something you'd like to wear tonight for the beach singalong." Jeanne gestured toward the heap of clothes on her bed. "You can keep whatever you choose."

Lizzy's mouth gaped open, "You mean it. Don't you? I don't know what to say. Thank you." She reached out and gave Jeanne a hug.

The girls turned toward a soft knock at the door; Jeanne opened to Ruby who walked over to Lizzy and touched her hair. "Your hair is fine like mine. I have some body shampoo that I think will be great for your hair."

"I dig it! You both are spoiling me!" Lizzy smiled widely. "I'll wash my hair now. Can you style it for me?"

"Sure. Let's get it done."

"Put on my housecoat, Lizzy. You can finish getting ready in my room," offered Jeanne gesturing toward her vanity.

Later, her wavy copper hair shiny and bouncy, Lizzy looked beautiful in a turquoise loose blouse and wide-leg pants with downward swaths of cream, turquoise, and maroon on a black background. Her coffee-colored eyes sparkled.

"I have a lot of sweaters so you can keep this one." Jeanne held out a maroon cardigan.

Lizzy grasped it and held it up to her face. "It's so soft. Thanks."

Jeanne wore a tan halter blouse and dark brown bell bottoms. Ruby chose pastels; a pink loose blouse and a pair of wide-legs covered with abstract pastel flowers.

"Girls, supper's ready!" Cynthia called. The three girls came down the stairs.

Nathan's brow lifted. "What have we here? Three very pretty girls, ayuh."

After eating their fill of salad, biscuits, and American chop suey, the three girls went to the door. Lizzy turned. "Thank you, Rev. and Mrs. Miller; I had a wonderful afternoon here."

"We enjoyed your visit. Come again soon." The girls left then and began the short walk.

"I feel like I have such wonderful friends." Lizzy put her arms around the twins as they neared the cove. Jeanne and Ruby turned their heads toward her and smiled.

At the beach, Jeanne and Lizzy went to speak with Brian while Ruby spread out their blanket. She looked up and met the eyes of the guitarist, who set his guitar aside and sauntered over to her side. "Hi! Ruby, I wanted to know if you and Jeanne would like to help us get the clambake ready Saturday."

"I'll ask. It sounds like fun, but I don't know anything about it."

Patrick touched her hand, and Ruby blushed when the gesture caused warmth to spread up her arm. "You'll learn, and I'll be there. I don't work on Saturdays and Sundays. See ya, Ruby. It's time to start."

Brian smiled broadly showing dimples. "Welcome everyone. I see some new faces with us tonight. Let's begin with a Gaither song. Strains of *Because He Lives* filled the cool beach atmosphere as puffins waddled around the singers. The light flashed and the foghorn sounded as the music played and the words rang out.

> God sent His Son; they called Him Jesus,
> He came to love, heal, and forgive.
> He lived and died to buy my pardon;
> An empty grave is there to prove my Savior lives!
>
> Chorus:
> Because He lives, I can face tomorrow.
> Because He lives, all fear is gone.
> Because I know He holds the future,
> And life is worth the living just because He lives!

Brian and Patrick moved over to the bonfire. Brian's wife, Julia, pulled up her lawn chair, and the participants picked up their blankets and came closer. *That thing about the papers… I forgot about it…Oh well…*

"Don't you know that every day may bring you some trouble? That's why we need to know the great troubleshooter. His name is Jesus, Yeshua in Hebrew. Our enemy, Satan, wants to accuse us and steal our joy. Jesus is praying for us from His throne. He lived here with us so we can know He understands all of our struggles. He was tempted but never sinned, the only perfect Son of God. When we don't know what to do, we can get down on our prayer handles and ask for His help. He will listen every time because He loves us unconditionally." "These verses in Philippians 2:5-8 reveal Jesus' attitude toward you and all other people who ever lived. 'Your attitude should be the kind that was shown to us by Jesus Christ, who though he was God, did not demand and cling to his rights as God, but laid aside his mighty power and glory, taking the disguise of a slave and becoming like men. And he humbled Himself even further, going so far as actually to die a criminal's death on a cross.' "He willingly took your punishment. Imagine you've been sentenced by a judge, and someone stands up in the courtroom saying he will take your place. That's what Jesus did for you. God's holy justice requires that sin be punished. Only the Son of God is without sin, and because of that, He qualified as the substitute for us. He rose from the grave showing us that He won the victory over Satan and sin. Will you give your life to him tonight? Tell him you're giving everything to Him. If you brought your papers where you wrote down your struggles and troubles, now's the time to throw them into the fire. If you need prayer, just come over to my wife and me."

Patrick played *Give it All* softly as blankets were vacated. Jeanne sat on her blanket listening to the crackling of the fire and the soft strains of the music. The cool, damp breeze seeped through her sweater making her shiver and draw the sweater closer as she folded her arms. She got up and went over to Julia. "Can we talk sometime?"

"Yes, Honey. I'm available after church Sunday. Are you?"

"I will be. Thanks." Jeanne smiled and went back to her place. All the other participants settled quietly onto their blankets.

"Julia is going to teach you the chorus to a new song written by Bill and Gloria Gaither last year. It's called *Something Beautiful*." Julia stood, and Brian sat beside her.

Everyone repeated the lyrics; then she sang the melody. Her mezzo soprano voice and her reverent spirit combined for a sweet atmosphere of the presence of God.

Something beautiful, something good,
All my confusion He understood.
All I had to offer Him was brokenness and strife,
But He made something beautiful of my life.

Lizzy's shoulders shook as tears splashed down her pink cheeks. Jeanne and Ruby moved closer to her. "My life can never be beautiful. I can't even remember how many foster homes I've been in, and the foster mother I'm with now is unbearable." *I believe that's true.*

"For those who feel the need to be baptized, stay after church Sunday for instructions with Pastor Nate. The baptismal service will be here next Thursday an hour before the singalong. We'll meet all the surfers tomorrow morning at 8:00. For those who didn't know about it, we're offering free surf lessons this summer. If interested, come and talk to me after we dismiss with prayer."

Jeanne was so concerned for Lizzy she was lost in thought. "Let's go, Jeanne," Ruby gently patted her shoulder. *What can Lizzy do? How can I help her?*

Chapter Seven

*N*EXT MORNING, THE FAMILY SAT around the breakfast table. Nathan grinned, "How would you like to go clamming this morning? Raymond will meet us at the clam flats in a couple of hours when the tide is going out. He'll show us green horns what to do. Ayuh. We'll dig 'em, cook 'em, and then eat 'em right there. How's that sound?"

Jeanne was vibrating with excitement, "I can't wait! I'll get ready after surf class."

Ruby and her mother smiled, "We'll get ready, my Dear." Cynthia kissed his cheek.

Later, clad in clam diggers, the family lifted their boots plodding through the squishy wet sand. Nathan carried the clam roller and two short-handled clam hoes.

Raymond waved, and then made his way over to them. "Gathah 'round and you'll know how to proceed. See heah, two will look for the steamahs, and two will do the diggin'. To find the clams look for breathin' holes. If yer not too sure a clam is in theyah, stomp yer foot neah the hole. If you get squirted, a clam is lurkin' about 6-8" down. Shout ovah to the diggah that you found one, and stay neah that hole. Diggahs, be careful to dig it up by settin' the hoe four inches from the breathin' hole, go down about 8", and pop up the steamah. Got that?"

Raymond also explained all they needed to know to do after the harvesting.

Jeanne and Nathan became enthusiastic diggers while Ruby and Cynthia spotted the clams' homes. They brought the clams to the roller, built with wooden slats and handles. When the roller was heavy with clams, Nathan carried it to the salt water and washed all the sandy clams thoroughly. Cynthia brought a canner over to him that he filled with some of the clams topping them with seaweed. The rest he left in the roller for the clam bake donation.

Jeanne and Ruby went to the back of the station wagon and brought out picnic necessities. Nathan built a fire in the fire pit beside the picnic table. He set the canner and a pan of butter on the grate. When the steamers were cooked, Raymond and the family gathered around for a lunch of steamed clams, shrimp sandwiches, coleslaw, and brownies. Seagulls trotted over sticking out their necks. Jeanne threw out some small chunks of bread that disappeared immediately. About six gulls swarmed around the table squawking for more.

"I have two questions." Ruby looked at her parents. "May I go for ice cream with Patrick after church?"

Her father winked. "Yes, my girl, I know him quite well. What's the other?"

"May Jeanne and I help prepare the clam bake tomorrow?"

Cynthia frowned, "I don't know. After all, we're the guests of honor."

"That's no mattah. Round these pahts it's all hands on deck!" Remembering his manners, Raymond added, "If I may say so, Ma'am."

Nathan nodded. "You girls can go."

* * *

After their succulent lunch, the family drove home. To their surprise, a woman and two children came out from behind the snowball bush growing by the flagpole. Cynthia went to the Native American woman, "Can we help you?"

"I hope you can. This was the only place where I could go when my husband, Golden Eagle, threatened to kill the children and me. My name is Pamela Locklear, Willow Tree, and my children are Laura and James, Blossom and Fawn."

"Come on inside and we'll talk." Cynthia touched Pamela's shoulder and smiled at the frightened children. "Don't worry. Everything will be alright. You're safe here."

After a private conversation with Willow Tree, Nathan shared the day's plans. "Mrs. Locklear and her children will spend the night and eat breakfast with us. Then, we'll all pile into the Chevy. You girls will get dropped off at Jake's, and your mother and I and the Locklears, will get on the ferry. Your mother and I are going to Bangor to shop for furniture. Pamela and her children will hop on the Greyhound to the Penobscot reservation in Old Town where her sister's family lives. Your mother and I will meet you girls at Jake's when we get back."

Very early the next morning, Jeanne woke up before dawn sweating and kicking off the covers. *I guess I know what the weather is today.* After changing into her thinnest cotton baby doll pajamas, she fell back to sleep. A knock woke her, and she stumbled to her door. "Hi! You're a sleepy head." Ruby looked adorable in a pastel flower print sundress, her silky hair in a smooth pageboy.

"I'll get dressed." Jeanne took a quick shower and pulled on a black and white geometric print sundress trimmed with red straps and three-inch border. She tamed her hair into a thick braid with red barrettes on both sides. *I hope the people will be nice.*

Chapter Eight

"WE'LL SEE YOU TWO LATER." Nathan opened the back door of the Chevy parked in the lot behind Jake's Fish Market.

The twins waved before hurrying over to one of the picnic tables. Maisie and Patrick smiled and came over to them. "Hi! Patrick said you were coming to help. He told me you've never seen cooking like this before." Maisie hugged the girls. She looked pretty in a yellow sundress with embroidered daisies across the top and around the bottom.

Patrick wore a yellow and orange tie-dyed tee shirt and khaki Bermuda shorts. He shook hands with the twins. When Ruby shook his hand, she met his gaze. Butterflies erupted.

"Native Americans taught the early settlers how to cook in a pit. Jake dug a pit back here for us islanders to use." Maisie gestured toward a large hole.

"How do you do it?" queried Jeanne.

Ruby pointed to the clams on the table. "We dug those yesterday."

Patrick grinned. "Thanks. The pit here is three feet deep and five feet across. See, it's lined with some big rocks. Mom and I came early this morning and built a wood fire on top of the rocks. It's been burning ever since.

I kept throwing the driftwood on it stoking it real good. Now we're letting it burn down.'

"Patrick will scrape out all the ash and charred wood. Would you girls please take these pails and get us some seaweed?" Maisie held out the pails.

"We'll be glad to, Mrs. O' Connor. We'll be right back," Jeanne answered. The twins swung the pails as they walked down to the beach. They scooped up the seaweed until the pails were so full the green fronds were hanging off the sides.

When the twins brought the seaweed, Patrick instructed, "We need to cover the red hot rocks with it. It will begin to steam like crazy." Jeanne and Ruby dumped their pails and smoothed the seaweed over the rocks with sticks.

"Over there in the wash tub are lobsters, clams, mussels, and quahogs. We'll dump all those and the clams you brought on top of the seaweed."

"We'll need to get some more seaweed and some salt water, and I'll soak this burlap sack. Ruby, would you like to come with me?"

"That'll be fine." When Ruby stood she was just slightly shorter than Patrick. *This could end up being a thing...*

"I could use some help wrapping these potatoes in foil. Usually, corn-on-the-cob goes in too, but it's unavailable until August." Maisie piled the potatoes on the picnic table. As they snacked and worked, their conversation covered several topics. Patrick and Ruby returned.

"Can I put the lobsters in?" Jeanne was up for a challenge. Patrick nodded, smiling.

Ruby looked doubtful. "Are you sure? It might bite or dig you with those claws."

Jeanne reached in and tried to grab a wriggly green lobster. It snapped its claws. She jumped back.

Patrick put on gloves and snagged one. "That's how it's done." In a short while, all the seafood and potatoes were in the pit. Water was sprinkled and seaweed was laid over the food. On top of everything Patrick spread out the wet burlap. "This will steam for two or three hours."

A truck pulled into the lot, turned, and backed in. "Here comes James and Maxine Parker with all the stuff we need to set up the welcome party."

Since Patrick and Ruby were sitting on the grass eating snacks and talking, Jeanne turned to Maisie. "I'm going to take a walk for a little while."

As she neared the end of the boardwalk, Jeanne spotted Violet and Lizzy making their way across the sand. She walked out to meet Lizzy who was wearing the blouse and pants Jeanne had given her. "Hi, Lizzy! Good afternoon, Mrs. Moore."

Violet nodded.

"Hi, Jeanne, let's take a walk over that way." Lizzy pointed toward the Southern end of the island. Not bothering to get permission, Lizzy grabbed Jeanne's hand and ran like a track competitor.

Once they were out of sight behind a rock outcropping, the girls slowed to a leisurely walk. "It's too hot to run so fast, Lizzy. What's up?" Jeanne's brow was furrowed.

"Just come with me. Okay? It couldn't have worked out better."

"What? We need to get back to the clambake."

"I want you to come with me somewhere." Lizzy turned with her hands on her hips.

Jeanne glanced at her necklace watch. "Can we get there in half an hour?"

"Yeah, we can." Lizzy started to say more but snapped her lips shut.

"What's wrong? We're friends, aren't we?" Jeanne stepped closer.

Lizzy didn't answer, and they walked on a trail through a wooded area. Beautiful asters and star flowers lined the trail. *Ruby could spend hours here.*

The girls came to a clearing. Spread out before them were vans and buses covered with graffiti of peace signs, flowers, scenes, and slogans. *This is a hippie commune!*

A bearded man wearing an open leather vest that showed his ripped muscles glanced up from his metal chair. He leaped up and sprinted to the girls. "Lizzy! You're here! You did it!" He grabbed her and swung her in circles. Who's your friend?" The man looked warily at Jeanne, who was staring from Lizzy to him, back and forth.

"Jeanne, this is my older brother, Marty. We're at the Aquarius Oasis commune. I'm staying here with him. You can go back now." Lizzy flicked her fingers.

"What? You're running away, Lizzy, and you brought me?" Tears threatened, and Jeanne's bottom lip trembled. "I can't believe this!"

"Promise me you'll keep my secret. Come visit sometime." Lizzy turned abruptly and left with her brother. They were laughing uproariously as they walked away, Marty's arm looped over his sister's thin shoulders. Jeanne watched while her friend disappeared into a rusty van. *I am in serious trouble. What can I tell Violet? Ruby? Mama? Daddy? God, help me! Please! How can I go back without Lizzy?* Jeanne sniffed, hot tears breaking free.

The area had a craggy shore, cliffs, and rocks; the commune was nestled in a valley. Jeanne stood atop a cliff. Behind the vans and buses were roughly constructed cabins and beach houses. Most people were indoors, but a few naked children were playing in the sand near the beach. *Six-six-six...* psychedelic strains of *Aphrodite's Child* swirled around. Jeanne groaned. *Ohhh...Lizzy! I have to go back to talk to her.*

Jeanne walked down the steep hill and sped over to the van. The van rattled when she pounded the door. Lizzy answered. "Come in. The three of us can talk."

Marty waved his hand toward an empty metal chair. "Lizzy has been telling me what a good friend you are to her. You deserve an explanation. We made the plan a few days ago. My sister and I hadn't seen each other for twelve years, since the day we first went into foster care. I picked up this van and came to the island last month when I got a job at the Maine Pink Granite Quarry. Last Saturday I took a tour of the lighthouse. That's when Lizzy and I saw each other. I sent her a letter asking her to come just as soon as she could get away." Marty paused. "I thought Lizzy would come alone."

Lizzy's voice filled with regret. "I'm sorry, Jeanne. Now you'll have to go back by yourself. Just tell them that I'm safe, and say nothing else. Promise me!"

"How long will you be here? You were coming to our sweet sixteen party." Jeanne choked up, stood, knocked the chair over, and flung the rusty door open. "Bye, Lizzy!" She scrambled up the grassy hill, slipping and sliding on the scattered gull feathers. *What am I supposed to do now? Going to the clambake is not happening. I should have brought my sweater.* Mist and a cool breeze swirled around her as the frothy waves struck the shore below with the sound of thunder.

"God, I feel so alone." Jeanne tipped up her face toward the cloud cover. "Lizzy is my friend, and she's left me with this secret."

Comforting warmth filled her heaving chest. <u>I will never leave or forsake you.</u>

Chapter Nine

JEANNE STRUGGLED UP THE STAIRS, dragged herself across the porch, and finally stumbled through the door. Ruby scrambled out of her chair and reached her twin just before she would have fallen Their parents rushed to help; Nate scooped her into his arms, laid her on the couch, and pulled an afghan up to her chin. No one spoke, but their relieved expressions gave Jeanne a feeling of assurance that she'd made the right decision to find her way home.

After resting there for an hour, a loud gurgle startled her to wakefulness. "I'm hungry!"

"Come out to the kitchen. We brought clambake leftovers, and I'll fix you a cup of chamomile tea." Cynthia smiled from the doorway.

Jeanne wrapped herself in the afghan, stood, and promptly plunked back onto the couch. "Coming, Mama!" On the next try, she managed to stand. She stumbled into the kitchen onto a chair. Her mother was at the stove warming the seafood.

"After you eat we'll catch up on your adventures." Cynthia turned and brought the tea kettle. She poured two cups and sat down across from Jeanne. *How will I explain this crazy day? Oh, this is a disaster…* "Trust me. I'll lead you." *Okay, God, here goes!*

"There's a lot to tell you, but it's getting late. I guess Daddy and Ruby are asleep."

Cynthia smiled and nodded her encouragement. "I'm not tired yet, Sweetie."

For the next hour, Jeanne shared everything that had transpired. Cynthia reached for Jeanne's hand. "I'll talk to your father tomorrow after church. Don't worry. Everything will work out. I'm just glad you're home. Let's head up to bed."

Jeanne, with a pained expression, groaned. "I'm afraid to face Mrs. Moore. What will I say when she asks about Lizzy's whereabouts?"

"I'll talk to her before she can get to you. Good night, Honey." Mother and daughter hugged. "Good night, Mama. Thanks for listening."

* * *

Even though there were puddles from the overnight downpour, the rays of sunrise proved that a clear Sunday was on the horizon. Jeanne sat on the window seat. A lump formed in her throat. *I'm scared...I'd like to pretend to be sick...I can't...It's the first service...I'm expected to be there smiling on the front row.*

Jeanne pulled out a peach maxi dress with a broomstick skirt. After dressing she sat at her vanity and brushed her long thick hair. She parted it on the side and fastened a wide gold barrette.

Ruby, wearing s pale green maxi dress, knocked and entered. "Will you tell me what happened?"

"I will this afternoon after I talk with Mrs. Smith." Jeanne hugged her twin and whispered, "Pray for me."

Cynthia was setting the kitchen table. "You girls look beautiful." She had fashioned a French twist and secured it with a sparkly comb. She wore a linen robin's-egg blue suit; the gently gathered skirt fell primly below her knees and matched a waist –length jacket. A white Peter Pan–collared blouse and blue pumps completed her outfit.

"Your father is already at the church. We will leave right after we eat."

Jeanne spoke in a low voice. "You'll just tell her Lizzy's safe. Right?"

Cynthia flashed a reassuring smile. "No worries."

Chapter Ten

"Jeanne, aren't you going to get out? Sunday School is starting soon." Ruby hesitated before climbing out when the car stopped in the church parking lot.

Dread filled Jeanne's heart. "I'm trying to work up the courage." She jumped at the bang on the hood but remained in place. *Violet!*

Cynthia heard the sound and halted. "Violet, why don't we walk together over to the side so we can talk?" She stretched out her hand.

Violet nodded and joined her. *Thank you, Mama!*

Jeanne entered the church and sat beside Ruby in the teen class; she didn't pay much attention to the lesson. *I don't even want to be here today...*

"Jeanne, why do you think Joseph was able to forgive his brothers?" Gregory Davis was asking her opinion. *I never give opinions...a good impression for my father is important though.*

"Well, he loved his brothers even though they had always been abusive to him."

"Good answer." After a few more minutes of discussion, Mr. Davis prayed and closed the class. All the classes tromped upstairs, entered the church, and sat with their respective teachers. Ruby went to the piano. The fifteen-minute Sunday School closing was jam-packed with birthday rituals of song and offering (the birthday person, according to their age, dropped coins in the slot of a bank shaped like a church), recitation of memory verses, and synopses of lessons; a rousing round brought the closing exercises to an end.

During the short break, Ruby and Jeanne moved up to sit silently beside their parents. Jeanne stared straight ahead until she turned to see who sat on her left.

Julia Smith smiled and lowered her voice, "I'm looking forward to our visit after church."

"Me too."

Ruby walked to the piano, and her father strode up to the pulpit and opened in prayer.

The worship band's symphony of piano, guitar, drum, fiddle, and slide trombone reverberated through the sanctuary. Three women led the singing; instead of hymnals, two ushers passed out song sheets stapled together. Jeanne sang along. *I like these songs.*

Pastor Nate ascended back to the pulpit. He looked approachable with his beard and mustache and open-necked burnt orange shirt. "Thank you for the welcoming spirit you have shown our family. We toured the lighthouse during a sunny day this past week, and we could view everything for miles from the top. I've always wanted to do that. It's just one reason why I'm happy to be pastoring on your island." He smiled as his eyes roamed over the sheep he was called to shepherd.

"For the next seven Sundays we'll look at the 'I ams' of Christ. This morning we'll examine John 8:12 where it's recorded that Jesus said, 'I am the light of the world:

he that followeth me shall not walk in darkness, but shall have the light of life.'"

His light shines everywhere into the world's darkness, people who are broken hearted, hopeless, and blind. He fills us with His light. Let's turn in our Bibles to Matthew 5:14-16. After the rustling noise subsided, he began reading. 'Ye are the light of the world. A city set on a hill cannot be hid. Neither do men light a candle and put it under a bushel, but on a candlestick; and it giveth light unto all that are in the house. Let your light so shine before men, that they may see your good works and glorify your Father which is in heaven.'"

"Now hear this same passage from *The Living Bible Paraphrased*: 'You are the world's light—a city on a hill, glowing in the night for all to see. Don't hide your light! Let it shine for all; let your good deeds glow for all to see, so that they will praise your heavenly Father.'"

"This morning we'll learn how we can be like the rotating beacon of light we see every night searching over tumultuous waves. We'll be inspired by Jesus' words in John 8:12, 'Ye are the light of the world,' We're Jesus people shining brightly, doing what Jesus did, blessing others with our kindest words and deeds."

Pastor Nate helped the people of Garden Isle understand the analogy of God's light inside them, even as a lighthouse illuminates and provides lifesaving direction. He closed his message. "Usually lighthouses are built high on a rocky shore. Jesus mentioned the lights from a city on a hill cannot be hidden and the light from a candle should not be hidden under a basket. As we head into a new week, I challenge you not to hide the light of Jesus' love but to let it shine!"

Ruby went to the piano, and everyone stood and sang *Pass it On* by Kurt Kaiser.

> It only takes a spark
> To get a fire going,
> And soon all those around
> Can warm up to its glowing.
> That's how it is with God's love
> Once you've experienced it.
> You'll spread His love to everyone.
> You'll want to pass it on…

Julia gently nudged Jeanne. "Would you like to ride with us to the Creation House? Do you want to eat lunch before or after we share?"

"I'll speak to Mama that I'll be with you after church. Can I eat after we talk?"

"Of course." Jeanne nodded and turned to tell her mother the plans.

When the last word of the benediction resounded with a hearty "Amen," Jeanne said good bye to her family and promptly left Seacrest Chapel without encountering any chaos. *I am a nervous wreck…talking things out is what I need to do though.*

Chapter Eleven

JEANNE WIGGLED TO THE BACK of the overstuffed chair; Julia sat across from her reaching for her hand. Wiping her hand on her skirt, Jeanne grasped Julia's hand. She held a tight smile.

"What is it, Honey? I'm here to listen."

Taking a deep breath Jeanne spoke each word like she was forcing each one to come out.

"Thank you, Mrs. Smith. I needed to find someone who'd listen."

"You are welcome. And please call me Julia." Her warm smile encouraged Jeanne.

Jeanne blurted, "I don't like being a preacher's kid!" The ceiling didn't fall in.

"That's understandable. I didn't like it very much either." Julia nodded. "Yes, I am."

"Wow! You really do understand. For starters, I don't know if I really am a Christian. I mean that I choose Jesus for a personal relationship. It's a role I have to play. Ruby and I were born into a ministry life style. We are both expected to be involved in the church work. Nothing can ever be shared about our family's problems. Ruby and I have endured torture from other kids just to see if they could make us do something not expected of a preacher's kid." Jeanne took a deep breath and let it out. Her face felt like it had been lit on fire.

"Go on, Jeanne Dear; what is said here stays here."

"Boys ran the other way when they found out what our father does, but last year I started dating a boy secretly. I wondered when someone would tell because I realized my behavior was always up for scrutiny. I miss Tony so much!" Unshed tears made her eyes burn.

Julia gestured toward the cans of Coke, "Let's stop a minute and have a drink." Between sips Jeanne and Julia shared their lives. They had seen more people's tragedy and true-life suffering than any child should ever witness. On the other hand, they had been a part of joyful occasions and laughed hilariously over missteps and misdeeds. "You've helped me uncover a lot of things I need to sort through. I feel I can have a heart-to-heart now with my parents and sister."

"I'll be praying for you that it goes well. It won't be easy I know."

Brian poked his head in the door. "Would you gals like to join us for barbeque?

"Ready?" Julia asked.

"Thank you for spending this time with me. I'm ready to eat now."

Young people were lined up to get red snapper hot dogs and burgers, Boston baked beans, and homemade sauerkraut. A separate table held a variety of desserts. Jeanne motioned to Ruby and cut in line. "Let's take our food over by the oak tree so we can talk privately."

The twins discussed Lizzy's situation. Jeanne had an idea. "Mama and I could go to see her Tuesday. I can bring her some clothes."

Ruby's eyes sparkled. "I start work tomorrow. I can buy a package of days-of-the-week underwear and a package of socks. I'll see if they have body shampoo and Yardley soap. I have some money from babysitting."

Patrick sauntered over to the tree and bent down by Ruby, "Are you ready to go get some ice cream?"

Ruby lifted a brow, and Jeanne nodded. "I'm ready to go with you, Patrick."

"See ya, Jeanne." The twins hugged. *Oh, she does everything right…not keeping secrets like me. I hope Tony has my letter…writes back.*

Chapter Twelve

AT BREAKFAST THE NEXT MORNING, Jeanne called a family meeting. Ruby was included since her training didn't start until 10:00. "I would like to talk to the family after breakfast." Jeanne's right foot reverberated against the kitchen floor.

"We can talk right here after we eat, before cleanup." Cynthia smiled.

"Okay." *They have no idea…*

Jeanne cleared her throat. "Yesterday when I talked with Mrs. Smith I realized that it was important to come clean with you."

"Go on, we're all listening, daughter." Nathan encouraged.

Words gushed out like a dam breaking. "I haven't seen that I can be a normal Christian. It feels like a family business and not a choice at all. I was born into a minister's family! I'm not too sure I've ever really made a choice to accept the personal relationship with Jesus. This has surprised you I know, but I am beginning to think about that." Jeanne's stare burned into her father. "Daddy, do you understand?"

"Yes, you need to make that decision. No one can make it for you. Let me know if you have any questions. Is there anything else?" Her kind, sweet father smiled.

Jeanne lifted her chin and braced both palms on the table. "I've been keeping a secret for the whole school year." Heat crept up her neck and face. She took a deep breath. "Tony Flores, you know from my class, is my boyfriend. Even Ruby didn't know I was meeting with him or that I lied when I said I was at Ina Thompson's."

Nathan stood up and crossed his arms. "Jeanne, you knew the rules of this family! No dating until sixteen! And-and you lied to your mother and me!" His voice was so forceful all the listeners jumped. Ruby shot a glance at her mother.

Jeanne succumbed to sobs, got up, and left the kitchen. She raced up the stairs and across the hall, and then catapulted from the door onto her bed. *Daddy and Mama are upset with me. They'll never trust me again.* She stretched across the bed sobbing for a half hour.

Cynthia and Ruby came to her door. Knock! Knock!

Jeanne's voice vibrated in frustration. "I have nothing else to say. Go away."

Cynthia spoke outside the door. "Ruby and I wanted to talk to you, Honey. Please!"

Jeanne flung the door open and saw that Ruby's cheeks were awash in tears. "This was such a mistake!" Jeanne gestured wildly. "I asked Jesus to forgive me, and I know He did. I feel Him close to me." She poked her chest.

Ruby drew her twin close in a hug. "Jeanne, that's wonderful. We're not mad, Jeanne. You surprised all of us, and Daddy feels badly for losing it."

"Let's group hug, girls." Cynthia put her arms around her twins. "Come back down."

Nathan was standing at the foot of the stairs as they descended. "Jeanne, forgive me. I want to understand. I love you." Her father caught her to his chest and smoothed her hair.

When the family was seated comfortably in the living room, Jeanne sucked in a breath. "I realize keeping the secret hasn't been fair. I love you with all my heart. Really, I felt lonely for a friend because everyone has always held me at arm's length because of the work you do Daddy. Finally, a boy paid attention to me even though I come from this family. I ask your forgiveness. I was wrong, and I'm ashamed." She swiped a tissue across her eyes and nose.

"You're forgiven," they answered in tandem.

"Can I talk now just to Mama about something different?" Nathan and Ruby nodded and left the room. Jeanne turned toward her mother. "I want to talk to you about Lizzy."

"What is it, Dear?"

"She has been in several foster homes for twelve years, but she'll be eighteen in October. I don't think she'll want to live in that "rusty, tiny bucket of bolts" for very long. I was thinking we could ask if she would want to live with us. She could share my bedroom. Her brother could visit her here."

"Well, we are licensed foster parents in Ohio. I could contact the DCFS in Ellsworth. Because I'm a qualified social worker, it could work out. Violet is still Lizzy's foster mother though. Do you think Lizzy feels threatened? Is Lizzy unhappy in her placement?"

"We could talk to Lizzy about this when we see her Tuesday."

"Okay, Jeanne. Give me time to think about it, and I'll need to discuss it with your father." Cynthia furrowed her brow and patted Jeanne's hand. "It will be all right, Honey."

Chapter Thirteen

"I CALLED MAISIE TO GET DIRECTIONS to the commune by car." Cynthia glanced at Jeanne.

"I'm glad because I'd never find my way through those rocks and crevices again. When we're closer, I think I can spot the area."

They drove a short distance and turned into the commune area that was nestled around the cove. Rocky cliffs towered above. "We'll do this." They stopped in front of the van. Jeanne grabbed the tote bag.

Cynthia put her hand on Jeanne's shoulder. "I'll sit on that bench."

Jeanne looked around while waiting for Lizzy to answer the door. A bare-breasted mother, her toddler standing by her side nursing, sat cross-legged on the grass in front of the nearest van. Her wrinkled maxi dress covered her knees and feet, except her toes poked out.

Disheveled and barefoot, Lizzy peeked out of the crack between the rusty hinges. She flung the door open. It sounded like a clanging cymbal. "Come in!"

The girls hugged. "Ruby and I thought you could use some clothes."

Jeanne had mixed and matched; Ruby pulled out a maroon skirt, cream-colored loose blouse, frayed bell bottom jeans, black skirt, wide belt, and flip flops besides the socks and underwear "Oh, thank you, and tell Ruby too. After this week visiting with Marty, I can't stay here." Lizzy looked away.

"What's happened?"

"A free-love man I didn't even know came up close to my face telling me he wanted it. I ran inside and locked the door. Besides, I was offered a joint. People are stoned all over the place. Most of the children and some of the adults walk around naked. I can't sleep with that psychedelic music breaking my eardrums." Lizzy was obviously frazzled and frustrated.

"My mother is here. Give me a minute to get her." Jeanne frowned.

Lizzy leaped to her feet. "This was our secret. You told!"

"Hold it! She and Ruby are the only ones who know! My mother would like to help you. She's over there on the bench." Jeanne came behind Lizzy plunking her back into the chair by pushing her shoulders. *Oh Lord, she has to say Mama can…*

"Okay, but give me five minutes to change and freshen up."

Jeanne ran to the bench and sat. "Lizzy wants to talk with you in five or ten minutes."

Cynthia turned to face Jeanne. "I've heard of these communes but have never visited one. See those two girls? That's Magic and Misty, sweet little girls. We were getting acquainted a few minutes ago. If their parents agree, I said we'd be happy to pick them up for Sunday School."

Cynthia listened intently while Jeanne reiterated her conversation with Lizzy. "She needs our help don't you think?"

"Yes, it seems that she does. I'm hoping she'll talk about what her life was like at the Moore's home. If she has issues with being there, I can work with the DCFS."

"Should I sit here while you go talk with her?"

"That may be best."

Cynthia kissed Jeanne on the cheek. Jeanne's palms were on her cheeks holding her scrunched up face. "You can go back in when our conversation is concluded." *That's Mama, always formal...*

After forty-five minutes, Cynthia left the van, and Lizzy stood just inside the open door. "Lizzy wants to know if you'd like to visit until Marty comes. He can drive you back home after work."

"May I?"

"I'll leave now, and you can stay. We'll expect you before suppertime."

Chapter Fourteen

Lizzy tried on the clothes modeling each outfit. Jeanne clapped. "They all fit you. I'm so happy! Can we walk on the beach?"

"Let's, but first I want to share some lunch. Fluffernutter sandwich and milk?"

"What is that?

Lizzy grinned. "That, my dear friend, is a sandwich made of peanut butter and marshmallow fluff. You'll think you've died and gone to heaven. It's that good!"

"Super! How long before I'll need to head home?"

"We'll have at least two hours after we eat."

Later, the girls got to know each other better, talking and giggling as they walked on the hard-packed sand near the sea. They had strolled out of sight when Marty pulled up in front of his van and went in.

Lizzy was nowhere to be seen inside; Marty went down to the beach and waved to her and Jeanne as the girls meandered around the bend. The girls waved back and soon caught up. Jeanne was flushed from the exercise; her wild hair was a victim of the sea breeze. "Hi, Marty." Jeanne reached up trying to smooth the corkscrews that made her look like she'd stuck her finger into a tangle of hot wires.

Marty chuckled, "Hi Jeanne. Lizzy, how was your day?"

"I'll tell you later. Could you bring Jeanne back home? I'll come too."

"That would pleasure me to do that for you. Probably enough walking for one day, huh? A friend of my sister's is a friend of mine." Marty winked, and Jeanne blushed.

The three came over the rise toward a yellow and black Carmen Ghia. "Your car is so cool! It's teeny weeny. Will we all fit?"

"We shall see. Jeanne, you take the passenger seat; Lizzy, climb in back."

Riding in the convertible, Jeanne could barely see with her hair blowing across her face. *So what about this mane of mine…* She directed Marty to the street and then the driveway.

Marty whistled, "Your house is bigger than I thought."

"It doesn't belong to us. A sea captain donated it to the church. We've lived here only about a week. Here comes Daddy."

Jeanne was ready to hop out. "Thanks, Marty."

"Not so fast. Let me open that for you." Marty unfolded himself and came around to the passenger side when he nearly bumped into Nathan who stepped back. Bowing slightly, Marty turned to the door, opened it, and extended his hand. "May I?" Jeanne took it and stepped out.

"Daddy, this is Marty, Lizzy's brother. Marty, this is Nathan Miller." The men shook hands while Lizzy got out.

"Let me tickle your fancy with some home-cooked beef stew. We'd be blessed to have you two join us for supper."

Marty looked at his sister who nodded. "Okay. We accept your kind invitation. I'll need to go get cleaned up first though."

Nathan smiled. "We won't start eating until you get back. Come meet my wife."

Cynthia and Ruby were standing on the porch; Lizzy and Jeanne joined them. After introductions, Marty drove away, and the others sat on the wicker furniture. A small table held a pitcher of icy pink lemonade and glasses. Ruby stood and served.

The Victrola was spinning with an Andrae Crouch record. The words floated through the open window. Jeanne had heard the top-listed song before. *That song again...I'll listen to it...*

> I've had many fears and sorrows.
> I've had questions for tomorrow.
> There's been times I didn't know right from wrong.
> But in every situation,
> God gave blessed consolation,
> That my trials came to only make me strong.
> Through it all, through it all,
> I've learned to trust in Jesus, I've learned to trust
>   in God...

<u>Trust me, and I will make all things beautiful in My time.</u> *I don't know how...help me...*

* * *

The Carmen Ghia appeared, and everyone on the porch waved. Marty, clean-shaven and dressed in a bright Hawaiian shirt and bell bottom jeans, was transformed. "I hope I didn't hold up supper."

Nathan shook his head "No man. You're right on time to dig in. Let's eat."

Jeanne felt embarrassed when Marty caught her staring and winked. He came to her and crooked his arm, "Shall we?" *A gentleman…nineteen isn't too much older…*

The new dining room furniture and hanging chandelier had been delivered and set in place earlier that day. The soup tureen, filled with beef stew, sat in the middle of the maple table with a basket of homemade yeast rolls and butter. Everyone stood behind the brocade upholstered chairs while Cynthia blessed the food. Marty went over to Cynthia and pulled out her chair. "Ma'am, allow me."

Is this guy for real? Is he just putting on airs?

Around the round table, easy conversation and laughter swirled until the last crumb of lemon meringue pie was devoured. "I'd love to help with the KP." Marty offered smiling and bowing.

"Thanks, but why don't you visit with my husband?"

Nathan responded, "Follow me to my office, right this way."

Later, everyone was seated in the living room. Marty was about to burst. "Jesus found me, and I prayed to receive Him. I felt a heavy weight lift off my shoulders."

"That's so amazing! I want to do that too." Lizzy's eyes were awash with unshed tears.

Ruby got on her haunches and took Lizzy's hands. "God loves you and has a wonderful plan for your life." She explained, "Jesus is the only one who made the way for you to be forgiven of your sins. He wants to come in by His loving Spirit. He's knocking; just open the door of your heart and ask him to come in and change your life. Will you? It's your decision to make." Lizzy looked around and nodded.

Tears streaming, Lizzy became one of the Jesus People right then and there. "I feel so clean inside." Brother and sister held each other with a joy they'd never known, tears mingling.

Chapter Fifteen

After breakfast Friday morning, Cynthia glanced down through her to-do list. You're both doing great on your new jobs. Your father and I are proud of our grown up girls, sixteen years old today. We'll start the party at 6:30. That will give you time to get home and gussied up. You've invited eight friends. Are they all coming?"

"Seven are definitely coming," said Ruby.

"We'll plan the barbeque for a dozen people. Pray for good weather; it's already cloudy." Cynthia turned toward the window.

Nathan entered the kitchen clutching the newspaper and some envelopes. "I think you got some birthday cards."

"Let me see those." Jeanne rushed to her father and held out her hand.

"Wait just a minute, girly." Nathan chuckled. "I'll dole them out. They're from Ohio, ayuh… ayuh." Jeanne rolled her eyes. *Sometimes, Dad, you act like a kid yourself.*

Ruby sat at the table, her hands clasped. Jeanne danced up and down. *Yes, this one with no return address must be from Tony.*

Finally, the twins took their mail to the living room settling into comfortable chairs. Jeanne propped her feet on a hassock and ripped the top envelope open. *A birthday card…a letter too from Tony…* Her smile faded while she read the letter.

Jeanne scrunched the letter and sent it flying like a missile. Then, she ripped the card into tiny pieces that fell to the floor like confetti. "I hate that Tony! He's forgotten all about me! What we shared meant nothing to him!"

Ruby set her own mail on the side stand and went over to her twin. "Look, Ina sent you something."

Jeanne reached for Ina's card. When she pulled out the card, a letter fell out. At the end of the newsy part she read, "Don't feel bad about Tony. I found out that when you were seeing him, he was with two other girls. You remember Rachel and Sally. I know you must be hurt, but believe me, he's not worth it. I miss you a lot. Maybe we'll see each other sometime in the future. Your friend, Ina" Jeanne read the shocking truth out loud. *I've been such a fool to trust him.* <u>Daughter, you've learned a great lesson.</u>

"Girls, I'm ready to drive you to work." Their mother jingled the car keys.

I have to get it together. Jeanne grabbed a tissue and leaped up clutching her purse. Ruby was already heading out the door. The ride to the A & W was silent; Jeanne got out and waved feebly. *Our birthday…but this is going to be a long day…*

Laurie met Jeanne as she came through the back door. "Hi, Jeanne. I can come to your party after all. Mom got another sitter for Tommy."

"I'm glad, Laurie." Jeanne's smile was forced. Woodenly, Jeanne participated in her training throughout the day.

Blake approached her putting his hand on her shoulder, "Jeanne, here's your pay for the days you trained. You may leave an hour early. We'll see you Monday. You've learned quickly and worked well with our team. Happy birthday and enjoy your party."

"Thank you, Mr. Richardson." Jeanne reached out and shook his hand. When she came outside, she saw Laurie by a car. "I'll see you later on." *I think I'll meet up with Ruby.*

During the short walk to the general store Jeanne's mood brightened.

"Hi, Ruby. I got out early." Jeanne sat at one of the empty tables.

"I'll be done as soon as I finish sweeping." Ruby walked slowly to the back of the store pushing a broom. Then she punched out and retrieved her purse.

"Hold up a minute!" Charlie called as the girls were getting ready to leave. He hauled over a bushel basket. "Two dozen con-on-the-cob that I impawted from outa state for yer sweet sixteen. It's all on the house. Ruby, here's your pay for the week. It looked like rain, but it burnt off for your pahty. Happy birthday to ya both!"

"We'll need to call Mama to come get us." They each took a wire handle and carried the corn outside. Ruby called from the phone booth on the right side of the parking lot.

Later, before the girls entered their rooms, Ruby said, "Why don't you go first? Your hair takes longer to dry. I bought you some shampoo especially for thick hair. Here."

After their bubble baths, the twins did their hair and dressed. Jeanne chose an off-white peasant blouse with tiny purple flowers and leaves paired with a green divided skirt; whereas, Ruby wore a loose pink blouse and hot pink divided skirt. Ruby wore her usual pageboy except she pulled her hair behind her ears and secured it with hot pink and white striped barrettes.

"Can I do something different to your hair?" Ruby smiled. "Trust me. You'll like it."

"Okay." When it was finished, Jeanne had two French braids across the back fastened with a green ribbon.

The twins stepped out into the backyard. Japanese lanterns were hanging, and the outdoor brick fireplace was already lit. Their father came around to them wearing his "Grill Sargent" apron and hugged his daughters. "Just sit your pretty big-girl selves down over there. No helping on your special day."

Soon all the guests, the Smiths, the O' Connors, Marty and Lizzy, and the co-workers, Beatrice and Laurie, left their cars and strolled to the backyard. The party got underway as they all stuck hot dogs into the fire, dished out salads, and ladled punch. The roasted corn-on-the-cob was a special treat. Conversations zigzagged around the table as everyone ate heartily.

Cynthia brought out homemade cake with pink frosting and a row of hearts all around the sides. Between the layers, strawberry jam had been slathered. The cake read, "Happy Sweet Sixteen," and sixteen candles were lit. "The A & W sent two gallons of Neapolitan ice cream." Nathan flattened the cartons and cut twelve slices. After all the birthday rituals, chairs were pulled back and the table was cleared.

Ruby turned to Lizzy, "I saw a job opening today on the community board."

"What is it?"

"The Seaside Inn is hiring a chambermaid."

"Groovy. I'm interested."

Their conversation was interrupted when Patrick picked up his guitar, He led the partygoers in several songs. The party ended after charades.

Marty pulled his chair over by the twins and his sister. "Thank you for inviting us." He whispered in Jeanne's ear. "You really look nice tonight, Miss Miller." *It turned out to be a good day after all.* <u>When you see Me work miracles, you'll see that I am who I said I am. I love you.</u>

"Lizzy, Jeanne and I would be so happy if you spent the weekend here with us."

Marty smiled. "That's a great idea. I'm sure you're a little cramped in my van and would welcome the change for a couple of days. I can drive you back to get your stuff."

Lizzy, jumped up and started to leave. "Will it be okay with your parents?"

Within earshot, Nathan leaned toward her. "What?" Jeanne asked permission.

"The more the merrier!" Nathan chuckled.

Chapter Sixteen

*M*ONDAY MORNING LIZZY DRESSED CAREFULLY for the interview at the B&B she'd set up earlier. It was a mite cooler so she chose the maroon sweater and pants with the off-white blouse. She slung her colorful brocade pocketbook over her shoulder. Her hair shone and hung in waves.

Cynthia drove the Beetle up and down a few streets until she stopped in front of The Seaside Inn. The spacious white clapboard house was surrounded by a variety of flowers that survive well in beach areas. There were several lawn chairs and green and white patio tables and chairs on a terrace facing the ocean; shiny green leaves sprouted from big decorated clay pots.

"Go ahead, Dear. I'll be waiting out here. Take your time."

"Thanks so much, Mrs. Miller. I'll be right back."

When Lizzy entered the lobby, an attractive, middle-aged lady met her. Her salt n' pepper hair was pulled back in a bun; she wore a soft pewter-colored dress with a black lace collar and pearl buttons down to the hem line. She smiled and her grey-blue eyes sparkled. "I'm Elizabeth Ruben, and you must be Elizabeth Raeburn. We can talk in the dining room." After taking seats in there, they discussed job particulars.

Before the interview ended, the proprietor gave Lizzy a strange look. "I have something to show you." She held out a picture. "Elizabeth, do you know who this person is?"

"That's my mother. I know it is. How did you get a picture of her?" Lizzy's knees were shaking. "I haven't seen her for a very long time."

"She's my niece. You were named after me. I'm so sorry I didn't get in contact with you sooner, but I only found out what happened two years ago. I didn't know where you had been placed." Lizzy and her great aunt hugged for a long while. They were both sobbing.

When she recovered her bearings, Lizzy found out that her mother had suffered a severe nervous breakdown and had spent ten years in the Augusta State Hospital. For the past two years she had been living in Blue Hill, a hop skip and a jump from Covington. Also, Lizzy told her great aunt that Marty lived and worked on Garden Isle. "This will be my first job, but I always worked hard for my foster mothers. I've done a lot of bed-making and cleaning."

Elizabeth touched Lizzy's hand. "We'd be happy to hire you this summer. I see from your application that you'll be eighteen October 15th. I have a thought. Since you're close kin, you could live here with us. We'd need to contact the social worker who placed you. Do you know who that might be?"

"No, but I know someone who can help us! I'll be right back!"

Lizzy politely shut the door but raced to the Beetle. Instead of getting in on the passenger side, she appeared at the driver's window. Cynthia rolled it down. "Lizzy! Did you get it?"

"Yes, I did, but wait until you hear what just happened!" She explained about her great aunt and asked if Cynthia would like to come in to meet her. The two women talked about the next steps to take, and Cynthia agreed to help as much as she could.

Elizabeth took Lizzy up winding stairs to a very beautiful Victorian-style bedroom. "This is the room I thought you might like."

Lizzy couldn't speak for a moment and swallowed. "Oh, Auntie! I don't like it; I love it! I never had a room this nice!"

"You'll be paid the usual salary, but you can live here. All meals will be included."

"When do you want me to come?"

"Just as soon as we can get things straightened out. You and I will go to meet with the social worker together where you can speak for yourself, and I'll make out the transference papers to place you with Ari and me." Lizzy threw her arms around Auntie Elizabeth.

"Can Marty and I go see our mother sometime?"

"Yes, Honey. Pretty soon we'll all go."

"When he gets out of work and comes to bring me home, I'll tell him everything." Elizabeth stood on the porch waving until the Beetle disappeared around the corner.

As Cynthia and Lizzy entered the parsonage, the phone was ringing; Cynthia ran to answer it. "Hello, this is Ari Ruben. I'd like to speak with Martin Raeburn." Cynthia assured him that they'd give the message to Marty as soon as he came in. "You're at the B&B?"

"Yes, that's the number. Thank you. Good bye."

"Good bye, Mr. Ruben."

Lizzy waited on the porch glancing at her watch. "You're finally here!" Unsuspecting, Marty grinned at his sister as he climbed onto the porch and slumped onto the swing.

"What's going on? Lizzy?"

His sister ran across the porch to him. "Our lives are about to change, Marty; that's what's going on! Shove over, and I'll tell you what happened today!" Lizzy tapped her lips. "Stay quiet, and don't interrupt me."

"I'm flabbergasted! I'd better call Mr. Ruben right now!" Marty knocked twice and Cynthia let him in.

Chapter Seventeen

After visiting with Elizabeth for a short while, Marty met Ari Ruben on the terrace. The man's brown hair was graying around his ears. He wore a Ralph Loren yellow polo shirt, khaki pants, and sandals. He smiled and held out his hand. "Martin, I'm Ari Ruben."

"I'm glad to meet you, Mr. Ruben. This was the first time I've seen Aunt Elizabeth for about fourteen years. How did you guys end up on Garden Isle?"

"My wife and I were living in Greenwich, Connecticut where both of us taught high school. We found an ad about this property being for sale in *The Down East Magazine*. Over an Independence Day weekend we came to look at it. There were a lot of tourists staying here. When we came home we crunched the numbers, sold our house in Connecticut, and bought the whole shebang!"

"I'm glad you came here. Why did you want to meet with me tonight, Mr. Ruben?"

"Say, you can call me Uncle Ari. I brought you here to present you with a proposal. I would like to hire you to work for us as a deckhand on our one-mast sloop. Monday through Friday I take groups of tourists out to watch for whales, porpoises, dolphins, seals, and puffins. There are usually weekend people catching the ferry to come here for that expedition. Being an observant Jew, I honor Shabbat; I need someone I can trust who can handle keeping the boat clean and watching for passenger comfort and safety, someone who will work well with Captain Robert Sweet. I would need you Saturday all day and Sunday from two to six. Also, the boat and the house will need maintenance from time to time. We have a nice furnished studio apartment above the boathouse that you can have rent free. Anytime you'd like, you can eat meals here in the dining room."

"It sounds great. Could I go up and see the apartment?"

"Let's go now. I'll warn you it hasn't been cleaned yet. No one has lived there since we bought this place." Marty followed Ari to the apartment.

"Thanks for showing me. This is very nice, Uncle Ari. I like this a lot."

"So what do you think? Are you accepting the offer?

"May I shadow someone for a couple of Saturdays before I'll have to be on my own? It's something I never did before."

"Patrick O'Connor worked here on Saturdays last summer. I'll offer the job to him for a couple of weeks. He's experienced and can help you feel comfortable with the job."

"May I call you tomorrow to let you know my decision after I sleep on it?"

"Of course, Marty, I'll wait for you to call."

Chapter Eighteen

"That went really well. Don't you think?" Lizzy, sitting primly on the Mercedes' leather seat, turned toward Aunt Elizabeth after they had left the DCFS. "Miss Gonzalez understood how I feel about living at the lighthouse even though it would be for only four months longer. I'm glad she's coming with us tomorrow. It'll be hard for me to go back there."

"We'll be with you, Honey, and we won't stay very long."

"Neither of you know what Mrs. Moore is like. I don't know what her problem is."

The next morning Lizzy and Jeanne rode with Elizabeth and picked up Christina Gonzalez from the ferry dock. Lizzy shook so much she clamped her mouth shut to keep her teeth from chattering. "I called yesterday and made the appointment; Mr. and Mrs. Moore are expecting us." The kind social worker reached back and tapped Lizzy's shoulder gently.

After they parked the car, Elizabeth walked beside Jeanne with Christina beside Lizzy. When they came to the door, Violet opened it before they knocked. "Well, well, Lollygag, you finally show your homely face here." Her voice was terse. "This girl ran away two weeks ago, and I…"

Christina interrupted. "May we please enter, Mrs. Moore? There's a lot for us to get done. This is Elizabeth Ruben." She turned to Jeanne. "Could you please wait over there on that bench? Lizzy will join you as soon as she finishes."

Jeanne frowned but left the door stoop and sat. Lizzy went to her sparse and cold bedroom and filled her backpack.

"You can drop it by the door. I'll take it to the bench when we get ready to leave." Elizabeth gestured toward the door.

"Use…Donald and I have been worried sick over the whereabouts of that…that girl." Violet shook her finger toward the door as Lizzy exited.

Elizabeth, lips tight, spoke. "The beautiful young lady you're calling *that girl* happens to be my great niece."

"That's correct, Mrs. Moore, this relative, has offered Elizabeth Raeburn a home." The efficient social worker rummaged in her briefcase pulling out a file folder. "I need you and your husband to read these documents and to sign them while we're here. Mrs. Ruben has already signed her section."

"It sounds just like a gift all wrapped up with a bow, but that girl is no precious gift for anyone. My husband will be back shortly." Without uttering another word, Violet left the kitchen. Flap! Flap! Flap! Flap! Violet's house shoes brought her to the base of the lighthouse. "Useless! Get yourself down here now!" The words bounced around inside the 90' cylinder.

"I'll finish cleaning this pane and I'll be down!" Donald hollered back.

While the two women waited inside engaging in small talk, Lizzy and Jeanne went to see Donald's grandfather in the cabin. Otis Moore smiled, his two gold teeth gleaming. "Lizzy! You came to see this old man!" He enveloped her in a hug. Jeanne knew that he was 102, in such good health he took no medicines, kept his own finances in order, and took the cabin cruiser for a spin at least twice a week. From his white hair and long beard to his chambray shirt and gray pants held up by wide orange suspenders. Otis Moore was not a bit discombobulated.

"Grand daddy, this is my dearest friend, Jeanne Miller."

"Welcome to my humble abode. You must be Pastor Nate's daughter." He sat and indicated that the girls sit. "How would you two like bottles of Moxie? Lizzy, could you get those out of the ice box? I'm thinking of playing a tune." Otis lifted a button accordion.

Soon Lizzy came back carrying three opened bottles. "Yes, please play us something." *Help Lizzy, Lord. None of this can be easy for her.*

Otis played and sang the chorus of "In the Garden."

And He walks with me,
And He talks with me,
And He tells me I am His own.
And the joy we share
As we tarry there
None other has ever known.

The girls sang along through all the verses. Lizzy wiped tears with her thumbs. "That's a beautiful song. Now I totally dig it, God's love for me I mean. You were right, Jeanne. 'He makes all things beautiful in His time.'"

"Would you girlies like to take a tour of Matilda?" To answer Jeanne's quizzical glance, Otis added, "I named my cabin cruiser after my darling wife who passed thirteen years ago."

"I guess we have some time before we have to go back," responded Lizzy.

Jeanne jumped up. "I absolutely love boats. You should see my collection of models."

Otis smashed on his captain's cap, quite fetching with the gold cording on the sides, and led the way out the back door and down a grassy slope. They all climbed into the cabin cruiser.

Surprisingly, the boat was spotless and smelled lemony. "Thank you, Captain Moore." Jeanne bowed slightly; that gesture brought a shine to the blue-gray eyes.

Lizzy looked out the porthole and saw Aunt Elizabeth step onto the rock path. She waved from the boat and signed that they were coming up in a minute.

"I won't be living here any longer, but that doesn't mean I won't be coming to see you." Earlier Lizzy had told him about her life's changes.

"Lizzy girl, I'll look forward to those visits. Bring this girl and her twin with you and we'll all venture out on the deep blue sea."

Kissing his dear weathered cheek, Lizzy said, "So long for now, Grand daddy."

Jeanne went into his outstretched arms, still amazingly strong. "It's been wonderful to spend this time with you."

The girls met the women by the bench. "Thank you for all you both did for me." Lizzy bent over and picked up the backpack and swung it over her shoulders.

"Would you ladies like to have lunch at the café? It's my treat." Elizabeth smiled.

They nodded enthusiastically. Christina answered, "I can come; I'll just take a later ferry. Thanks, but I can pay for my own.

"I insist." Elizabeth patted her purse. The four savored their lunches.

After dropping Christina off at the ferry dock and Jeanne at work, Elizabeth headed to the B & B. She turned on the radio, state-of-the-art with stereo speakers. "This is Breaking News that just came in! There's been an accident at the Pink Granite Quarry on Garden Isle. The injured have been airlifted to the Eastern Maine Medical Center in Bangor."

"Auntie, could we go to the Millers? I need to find out about Marty."

"Of course we will." When the Mercedes pulled into the driveway, they found Ruby pacing on the porch. She ran out to the car. "Lizzy! Marty got hurt at work! He's in the hospital! We're going there now! You can ride with us!"

"Go ahead, Sweetie, I have to get back to the B & B for people who'll be coming in shortly." Elizabeth held Lizzy close. Turning toward Cynthia, she said, "Please keep us in the loop. We'll pray." Soon the car disappeared around the corner. Ruby and Lizzy sat on the porch swing.

Cynthia went inside and phoned the A & W. "May I please speak to Jeanne Miller?"

After her mother explained what they knew and their plans, Jeanne approached her manager. "My family wants your permission for me to leave for an emergency trip to Bangor."

"We'll cover for you. Not to worry. Go ahead."

God, I pray Marty will be alright...I care for him, but I know you care more than me.

Driving the Chevy off the ferry ramp, Nathan asked, "Would any of you mind if I turned on some inspirational music?" No objections.

A deep male voice announced, "Tracy Dartt has released a new song that is sure to be an inspiration. For your listening pleasure, here's *God on the Mountain*."

> Life is easy, when you're up on the mountain,
> And you've got peace of mind, like you've never known.
> But things change, when you're down in the valley,
> Don't lose faith, for you're never alone.
> For the God of the mountain, is still God in the valley.
> When things go wrong, He'll make them right.
> And the God of the good times, is still God in the bad times.
> The God of the day is still God in the night.

Father, I trust you to help Marty and Lizzy.

High Tides, Low Tides

Chapter One

"Have you heard anything yet?" Brian asked as he and Patrick strode into the emergency waiting room.

"Yes, the nurse said the emergency surgery is going well but may take another hour. There is more imbedded gravel than they thought at first." Nathan.

Patrick greeted everyone and stopped in front of Ruby. "You must be hungry. Would you like to go to the cafeteria?"

"Yes. First, I need to let Mama and Daddy know."

Crossing to the sectional, Patrick asked, "Could we bring food or drinks to anyone?"

Cynthia shook her head. "You go ahead. We'll get what we need from the vending machines."

Glancing up from his book, Nathan added, "Be back in an hour. We're joining for prayer then, and we should be hearing from the doctor."

Ruby hugged Lizzy and whispered, "Marty's in God's hands. Everything's ok."

Later, Patrick and Lizzy sat silently in the cafeteria eating. Patrick broke the silence. "What are you thinking?"

"I was thinking about Garden Isle having 213 species of migrating birds and 526 different bushes and flowers."

Patrick chuckled, "You've told me that bit of trivia umpteenth million times. What are you thinking here?" He tapped his chest twice.

"Okay, okay, you know I'm a bit shy. I was thinking about being Jeanne's twin and how our relationship is changing."

"Did you want to talk about it?" Patrick touched her hand. "I'll listen."

"We have always been close. When we were little, we were always together. Until we moved here we shared a bedroom. I can't get used to us sleeping in separate rooms. There began to be different hobbies and interests when we were nine. Jeanne started spending time with our Uncle Jerry while he worked on his antique car, and she began putting together model cars and ships. I started piano and porcelain doll lessons and spent time sewing doll clothes and learning to cook."

"Don't be embarrassed." Ruby's neck turned red. "Let's just say that when we were eleven, Jeanne beat me to the puberty milestone. After that, she started getting a little bossy, which I didn't like. I was 5' 10" tall by the next year. Boy oh boy, was that awkward! I was taller than anybody in our class. Jeanne made friends easier than I did, and so I felt left out in Junior High. I always have been more interested in school. Don't think I'm bragging. I have always gotten better grades, and I think she may be a little jealous." Ruby stopped and drank more cranberry juice. "We'd better eat this before it gets cold."

"I'm eating while you're talking, but let's dig in now. You can't talk and eat at the same time. I'd like us to be able to visit the dessert bar before we go back up." The couple finished eating and returned to the full waiting room; the family members of two other injured co-workers had also settled in there.

"Would you all like to join in prayer?" Pastor Nate reached out both arms to indicate joining hands in a circle. After everyone had grasped hands, he prayed, "Father, we join together to pray for Marty, Steve, and Frank. May they know your peace and watchful care over each of their lives. These families need your strength and comfort. We pray for wisdom to be given to the doctors. We pray that recovery will be swift. In Jesus' name we pray, amen." A doctor swung the door open when the prayer ended.

Hands clasped behind his back, the surgeon, still wearing scrubs, spoke, "I'm Dr. Gerard. May I please speak with Martin Raeburn's family?"

Lizzy stepped forward. "It's just me, but this is my pastor and his wife. May they come with me?" The doctor nodded, and they left the room for a private consultation.

Ruby and Patrick moved toward the sectional. Jeanne's arms were folded and her face wore a scowl. She spat out her angst. "We're in an emergency here, and you two are dating!"

Patrick scowled back and set her straight. "Wait a minute there! We were hungry and just got a bite to eat. That's unfair!"

Ruby implored her twin with her eyes. *Please Jeanne... Give it up.*

"Oh, all right. Sit here." Jeanne slid over to make room for them.

Jeanne turned toward Brian. "Do you know what happened at the quarry today?"

Brian brought a folding chair, turned it backwards in front of the sectional, and rested his arms on the back. "Yes, I went to the quarry and spoke with the foreman. The conveyor rail lost power that made the carts full of blocks crash into each other. Three men who were working nearby got injured. I asked about Marty; apparently he rolled to the right side where he got the brunt of breaks, scrapes, and lacerations. The good news is that he didn't get hit by the blocks that pitched forward. I think the surgery took quite a while because he had embedded gravel."

Lizzy and the Millers reentered. "Thank the Lord he'll recover." Nate informed the others. "He has a broken collar bone and wrist, and three broken ribs on the right side. He'll be here for a week, and it will be a couple of months until he'll have a complete recovery. Lizzy can go into the recovery room. After he's admitted to his room, he can have two visitors at a time for short periods."

Lizzy bent over pressing her hands on her knees. "I'd like to stay here with Marty. The doctor said they'd set up a cot in his room. The hospital will bring me meals. I called the Inn; Aunt Elizabeth is coming to see Marty tomorrow and will bring me back home."

"Do you want me to come into Recovery with you now?" Jeanne asked.

"Would you? I'm a little nervous about seeing him for the first time."

"You can stay no more than fifteen minutes. We need to leave right away to catch the 5:30 ferry to Garden Isle." Cynthia hugged Lizzy. "Please let Marty know we'll visit him tomorrow."

"Patrick and I will be catching that one too." Brian put his hands on Lizzy's shoulders. "There are high tides when everything is going well and low tides when they aren't. When the tide's up, everything is beautiful; the waves are foamy and the sounds are rhythmic and melodic. But the low tide reveals what's underneath, wet sand covered with litter, abandoned towels, broken shells, and lots of gobbledygook. Isn't that right? Lizzy Dear, Jesus is with Marty and you during this low tide. I can't imagine how disappointing all this is for both of you and just when the high tide had rolled in. Remember, our Lord does a wonderful work in our hearts even during the lowest times. Let Marty know Julia and I will be praying and will come to visit him."

Chapter Two

"You're not going to believe what happened today!" Lizzy held a tall glass of lemonade in one hand and a ginger cookie in the other.

From the porch swing, the twins in unison asked, "What?"

"Marty and I had finished with our breakfast trays, and the nurses and doctors had left when we heard a knock. I answered it. Guess what?"

Jeanne fluttered her hand to signal Lizzy to get on with it.

"Aunt Elizabeth had picked up our mother! What a surprise! Mama looked so much older, but she had the same sweet smile I remembered when I was five. She burst into tears when she looked over at Marty. Jeanne, you saw him yesterday. We were all sobbing. Mama told us how sorry she was for all we had gone through. Marty and I told her it wasn't her fault. There was a lot of love in that room!"

"We had family time until Marty needed to rest. After lunch in the cafeteria, Auntie drove Mama back home. She has a nice condo with a red cedar hedge. Pretty flowers line the walkway. I noticed pictures of Marty and me on top of her bookshelf in the living room. The rows of spices on the kitchen wall gave away that she likes to cook. In fact, Mama invited my aunt and uncle, Marty and me to come to dinner when Marty gets better."

"We're so happy for you!" Jeanne leapt from the swing, almost knocking Ruby out, and gave Lizzy a smothering hug.

"I just saw the Mercedes heading this way. I can't wait to sleep in my new bedroom tonight, and I'll start my new job tomorrow morning. Love ya! See ya!" Lizzy went to Ruby and they shared a goodbye hug.

After supper, Nathan looked across the table. "Your mother and I have been invited to a minister's conference in Portland. It'll start tomorrow evening and end Saturday afternoon. We can trust you girls to hold down the fort. Ruby, may I ask you to type my sermon notes? I'll leave them on the desk by the Royal."

"Yes, I'll do that, Daddy."

Cynthia consulted her to-do list. "Could you girls water the flower garden? There's plenty of food, except we need milk and eggs. Ruby, could you bring those after work? And Jeanne, can you bring home some A & W root beer? We'd rather you girls not use the grill while we're gone, but if you'd like to thaw some chuck steaks, we can have a barbeque for supper Saturday. Please wash eight potatoes and boil six eggs for potato salad."

Nathan rose from the table chuckling, "This will be a little romantic getaway for your mother and me. Thank you both for helping. I know this is short notice, but we just got the invitation in the mail this morning. We're going up to pack and get everything ready."

This is nothing new. Last minute events and emergencies is our life. We've always helped. I guess I'm proud of us twin super-girls.

Chapter Three

*R*UBY SAT AT THE DESK facing the typewriter. After rolling in the paper and setting margins, she glanced over the notes. *Interesting...*

Title: Get a Life

Main point: Jesus said, "I am the way, the truth, and the life"

Introduction: The story of two lives

Two contemporary men and their descendants: Jonathan Edwards and Max Jukes

<u>Max Jukes was an atheist, married to an ungodly woman.</u>

540 descendants: 150 criminals, 100 alcoholics, more than half of the women were prostitutes, 7 murderers, and many died in the poorhouse. This family has cost the government millions.

<u>Jonathan Edwards was a humble Christian, married to a godly woman.</u>

1,394 descendants: 13 college presidents, 65 college professors, I US Vice President, 3 US senators, 80 public officials, 30 judges, 100 lawyers, 60 physicians, 75 military officers, 100 ministers and missionaries, 60 prominent authors, and 295 college graduates that were governors and ambassadors. None of them cost the USA one penny.

Read John 14:6 and John 10:10

Prayer

Ruby typed details for three points: 1. The Way, 2. The Truth, 3. The Life then, she typed the concluding remarks and illustration.

St. Patrick's Life Prayer:

I arise today, through God's strength to pilot me,
God's might to uphold me,
God's eye to look before me,
God's ear to hear me,
God's word to speak for me,
God's hand to guard me,
God's shield to protect me…

Br-i-n-g! Ruby reached for the phone. "Hello, Miller residence. May I help you?"

"May I speak to Revrund Millah? It's of vital impotance."

"He's away until Saturday. I'll give him your number when he comes home."

Ruby wrote his name and number on a memo pad.

Jeanne opened the office door a crack. "I made us some popcorn if you're ready to watch television," Ruby left the office and settled on the couch beside Jeanne.

"This is cool to be here together. I'm going to grab a couple of Cokes."

Br-i-n-g! "Hello. Miller residence. Jeanne speaking."

"Hi! May I speak to Ruby please?"

"Ruby, Patrick wants to speak with you. Don't take long."

After the greetings, Patrick asked, "Can I come see you in a few?"

"What if we make it tomorrow night instead?"

"I guess it can wait. I want to ask you something in person. Is 7:00 okay?"

"Yes, that'll be fine."

"Good night, Ruby."

"Good night. I'll see you tomorrow night." *I want to be with Jeanne. We need this time.*

Chapter Four

BEATRICE GIGGLED NERVOUSLY. "I THINK he likes me." She was telling Ruby about the very tall man. (definitely over 6'6") who had come into the store to buy a magazine. "He looks like a prize fighter with those huge muscles and blonde crewcut. Those green eyes pierced right through me when I checked him out."

"Your father won't be happy if we take too long a break," cautioned Ruby.

Beatrice's blue-black hair and her pale blue eyes was a striking combination. Ruby and Beatrice, who was fifteen, had become more than co-workers; they were friends. As the girls returned to work walking side-by-side, it was difficult to tell them apart from the back.

Later, Ruby came in the house lugging a paper sack. *I'm nervous about our talk.* "Jeanne, let's have leftovers tonight. Patrick is coming at 7:00 and I need time to get ready."

Jeanne rolled her eyes. "We wouldn't want to keep him waiting, would we?"

Ruby changed the subject. "Have you heard how Marty is?"

"Lizzy said he's not in as much pain. Sunday afternoon Mrs. Ruben is bringing us to see him. We're getting their mother on the way there."

After the twins ate and cleaned up, Ruby went upstairs and got ready. She chose a baby blue sundress with white polka dots and a lightweight navy blue sweater.

Ten minutes before 7:00, Ruby switched on the porch light and sat on the swing. *We'll have some privacy here. I wish I knew...*

Jeanne smiled and positioned the tray on the wicker table. "I brought you and Patrick some strawberry-rhubarb pie. If you want it heated with vanilla ice cream, just holler." She hugged Ruby and left.

Patrick stepped out of his Ford 4x4 carrying a bouquet of yellow roses and baby's breath. He took two steps at a time and stopped. "Ruby, you're beautiful."

It took Ruby a second to respond, "Hi, Patrick. You can sit here beside me." She blushed as she patted the seat beside her.

Patrick held out the flowers, "These are for you." He cleared his throat.

Ruby stood up, "Thanks, they're lovely. Let me put these in a vase. We have this pie. Would you like to have it heated with some vanilla ice cream on top? If you'll get the door, I'll be right back."

Momentarily, she returned with two pieces of pie ala mode.

Patrick forked a generous portion. "This is so-o-o good. Did you make this?"

Ruby blushed. "Yes, I did. You told me once this is your favorite." he turned and smiled.

"I wanted to ask you two questions."

"What are they, Patrick?"

"Would you go steady with me? Will you be my steady girlfriend?" He reached for her hand and turned it palm up. "Will you wear this friendship bracelet?"

"Yes, I will. My father already said he approves of you." Patrick took the opportunity to slip his arm across the back of the swing.

"What's number two question?"

"It's something I thought of that we might want to do together. I already shared my idea with Pastor Nate and Brian. On Sunday evenings I thought we might have a children's ministry at the commune. Several of the children want to come to Sunday School, but their parents are concerned about the police finding out what is going on down there. What do you think?"

"You can count me in, but we'll need to prepare so we do this right."

Chapter Five

S'MORES COMPLETED THE BARBEQUE AS the Millers gathered around the backyard bonfire. "Daddy, you got a call from Clyde Edwards. He said it's of vital importance. Here's his number." Ruby reached into her pocket and pulled out her memo.

Grasping it, Nathan went inside to call. When Nathan returned, he laughed in pure delight. "We're going to have a wedding. Ayuh. Clyde Edwards and Marlene Sweet want to get married next Saturday. Tomorrow afternoon they're coming to see me to work out details."

"That's quick." Cynthia's eyebrows lifted up.

"He said he's going to basic training at Fort Dix, New Jersey in a month and will probably be deployed to Viet Nam afterward."

"I'll talk to Flo about the decorations and the preparations for the reception." Cynthia offered.

Nathan asked, "You do know that Florence Sweet can be a little difficult don't you?"

Cynthia nodded. Jeanne spoke for the twins. "Ruby and I are happy to help anywhere we're needed."

Almost every evening that week, the church ladies met with the bridal mothers to make centerpieces and to plan the details of the reception.

Ruby, always analyzing, observed the bridal mothers' personalities.

Gertrude Edwards is not willing to adapt to others' ideas. Florence Sweet feels she does everything right and trusts no one else.

In spite of the rocky preliminaries, come Saturday the wedding was held in the Edwards' door yard. Stacked lobster traps provided the backdrop for the nuptials. Marlene, wearing her mother's gown, alighted from a red pickup bed. Clyde was on hand to lift her out. Her mother handed over the bouquet of lupines and lemon lilies. Guests sat in rows of folding chairs. Laura, a tall, broad-shouldered woman wearing a royal purple dress, sang" *I Love you Truly*" in a falsetto voice that wrangled the nerves. The ceremony was sweet, and Clyde shyly pecked his bride's lips. Charlie took pictures with his newfangled Kodak.

Tables were brought out and the chairs were arranged around them, the plastic tablecloths were spread out, and the centerpieces were placed just so. Then, there was the cake. It looked like the Leaning Tower of Pisa. It was a pale shade of gray with three layers piled together. Tiny silver balls graced the edge of each layer, and a plastic bride and groom teetered on top.

The food was delicious, and there was plenty to go around, but the cake and frosting were heavy with lard. Gertrude was proud of her culinary creation. *Hasn't she heard of Crisco?*

There was no booze or dancing since Christians refrained from all worldly amusements. Gifts, opened by the bride and groom, were passed around. It was a different custom to be sure, but there had been no time for a bridal shower. Yes, guests passed unmentionables. Ruby blushed beside Patrick. He smugly looked straight ahead. *Oh brother!*

Jeanne stepped over to Ruby, "I'll see you later. Mrs. Ruben just arrived to take Lizzy and me to see Marty. If the doctor gives his permission, he'll be discharged Monday." *She's forgetting Tony. I won't see much of her once he's home.*

Chapter Six

*I*NDEPENDENCE DAY WAS A BIG deal on Garden Isle in 1973. The community would be congregating behind the general store for food, games, and speeches. Ruby and Beatrice were Charlie's assistants for the elaborate set up.

When everything was ship-shape, Beatrice tapped Ruby on the shoulder. "Let's go to my house now to get ready."

"I'll go get the bags." Ruby offered. She and Beatrice had bought matching outfits that day to wear, since they were helping Charlie host the party.

Charlie came outside looking festive in his Abraham Lincoln style hat with vertical red and white stripes, a band of white stars on a blue background, and a blue brim. He wore a white shirt, red bowtie, and blue blazer; his trousers were bright red with red and white striped cuffs. "Daddy, you look so, so patriotic…and cool."

Later, the friends came back to the store wearing frayed-bottom jeans and tie-dyed shirts. Ruby's was blue and white, and Beatrice's was red and white. Their sandals flapped on the floor. "We're here to get everything ready, Daddy." Beatrice reached for the bags of chips.

"How's my girl? Charlie winked at his daughter. "Maisie O' Connor dropped off this sheet cake earlier."

"That's cool the way she arranged the raspberries and blueberries to look like a flag."

The threesome worked together finishing with a little time to spare. They admired their red, white, and blue decorations while they lit all the candles.

Soon, families arrived choosing tables and settling excited children. They all brought salads and desserts which Ruby and Beatrice received and assembled on the serving tables. One small table held a humungous punch bowl filled with red punch swimming with orange slices.

The Chevy pulled in. Sebastian hopped out and helped an older lady. *She must be his Grandmother.* Ruby went to greet them and her family.

The Millers and the Smiths sat at a reserved table. Ruby strained to hear the low conversation. Brian sipped his punch. "How did things go at the convention?"

"It was an experience in the Lord I'll never forget. The host church was Crossroads Church of God in Christ that has a humble, but strong shepherd, Ebenezer Swain. I've never seen anyone play the piano like his wife, Corinne. Right, Honey?"

"Oh yes. And the steel drum orchestra blessed us. We hope to have them bless Seacrest in the near future."

"We've invited the Swains to stay with us a week from Saturday night and to minister in the Word and music Sunday morning." Nathan smiled. "I think we'll be close brothers."

"Do you think some people will object? We certainly don't." Brian and Julia leaned forward. "In fact, we'll look forward to their ministry."

Nathan continued. "Speaking of Church people, Crossroads people all stood at once when Ebenezer took the pulpit; they stretched out right arms and shouted in unison, 'God bless the man of God!' I've never witnessed clergy being given that much respect. Excuse me. They're calling me to bless the food and the event."

After the prayer, voices blended in singing *God Bless America* while children waved their small flags in one hand and held their sparklers in the other. The community families filled their plates and sat to eat and chat. There were skits, speeches, and games.

Ruby and Beatrice plopped into lawn chairs after the last car had disappeared. "That was fun, but now we have to clean up." Ruby wiped her brow with a napkin.

Jeanne and Lizzy approached. "Why don't you two take a little break? Lizzy and I can take it from here." Jeanne hugged her twin and smiled.

The sunset of brilliant red and orange hues was fading and a cool breeze rustled leaves. In the gathering darkness, everything was a silhouette. "Okay, we'll take a walk on the beach for a few minutes." Ruby and Beatrice pulled on their jean jackets. "Thank you. We'll be back in a few."

A full moon illuminated their way as the girls walked on the hard-packed sand.

Chapter Seven

As they approached the lifeguard station, the girls suddenly stopped. There was a flashlight beam pointed at them. Arms reached out and grabbed them pulling them to rock-solid sweaty, smelly chests. "A-R-R-R!" Beatrice screamed. Ruby froze.

"You can scream all you want to, but no one will be able to hear you. "The engine of the flying boat is revved up already to bring you..."

Beatrice began to struggle, kicking and biting. "Let me go, you beast!" *With that red afro and thick red mustache, he does look like a beast. He must be 300 pounds of muscle.*

Ruby felt the cold hand grasping her arm and fainted. When she revived, beady eyes stared down at her. "You're coming with us. Now! We gagged that loudmouthed friend of yours!" *That voice sounds familiar. It's him from the store!*

"Lord, help us!" *Beatrice and I are being kidnapped.* Ruby whimpered softly.

<u>I will not leave you defenseless nor loosen my hold on you.</u>

"I'll end up breaking an arm if you won't let me hold your arms down. He wouldn't be happy if we brought him damaged goods." Beatrice' captor had a bite mark on his forearm.

Ruby's hands were tied, but Beatrice's chest and waist was wrapped with the thick rope. Both girls were slung over broad shoulders like sacks of grain and plunked onto the back seat of the sea plane. They scooted closer together, shaking; their teeth were chattering.

At the highest speed and skipping over the waves, the plane tipped from side to side like a teeter totter. It halted with a jerk at a rocky shoreline. *I hope we don't have whiplash.*

Mission accomplished, the crewcut man spoke soothingly, "Sorry for earlier. We need to get along since we'll be occupying the same space for quite a while. My name's Tom and this is Guy. We'll untie you so you can wriggle through the crevices to your new home."

Trembling from head to foot, Ruby asked, "Where are you taking us? Everyone will be scared when they find us missing, and they'll come searching high and low."

"No one will find you in this place. The Indians lived here for one hundred and fifty years." In the light beam emanating from the sea plane, Ruby could see Guy's pocked face and bloodshot eyes; spittle formed around his mouth as he informed the girls of their helpless plight.

"Hold onto this rope, and we'll guide you safely to the Great Light Kingdom. The master will be happy to receive such pretty young ladies." *Oh Dear God! We're being taken to a cult!*

Both girls stumbled over rocks and sticks more times than they could count, and Ruby cut her right foot on a sharp rock. By the flashlight beam, a large house with an arbor roof came in view. *It does look like a tribe built this.*

"We're here at your new home. If you're real nice to him, he'll be nice to you."

Beatrice gritted her teeth. "Never! No never!"

Ruby took a different tack saying with an insincere smile through gritted teeth, "Of course." Tom unlocked the door and pushed the girls inside.

The guru came toward Ruby and Beatrice grinning through his thin purple lips. He had thick black hair that came to a point on his high forehead, straight-across eyebrows, mustache, and long beard. His nose was bulbous, and from his pointy ears hung three–hoop gold earrings. Strands of colorful beads hung below his double chin and fat neck. Over his girth he wore a bright yellow full-sleeved shirt and black genie pants tied with a wide white belt. His squinty green eyes assessed the newbies. "Welcome to the Great Light Kingdom family. We'll have the weddings tomorrow after you've had some rest." *Dear Lord, help us!*

Beatrice was frantically pointing at a frame while being careful that the gesture was for Ruby's eyes only. Two of Father Yod's Ten Commandments were beautifully written in calligraphy.

Obey and live by the teachings of your Earthly Spiritual Father.

Each morning join your vibration with the ascending currents of the Universal Life Energy using the keys that your Earthly Spiritual Father has taught you.

Ruby was frightened. *How can we leave this evil place?* Your Heavenly Father will make a way where there seems to be no way.

The girls were ushered into a large room. "You're my numbers six and seven. Seven is the number of complete perfection. Tomorrow I'll issue your new names. I am Father Yuri; in due course I will show you how to receive divine light from me. Tom will bring your white dresses you'll wear at all times." Yuri turned on his heel and left.

Tom unlocked a door. "Here's the bedroom you're sharing with five other girls." The small room was jam packed with the seven beds. The beds were lined up in two rows with a space between of three or four feet. There was about two feet between the beds that were wooden with a thin mattress and one flat pillow on top. A built-in drawer was empty. A moth-eaten green army blanket was folded at the foot of each of the beds. There were no sheets or pillowcases so ruby spread out the blanket and laid on it. *I'll wake up soon from this nightmare.*

By the sounds of the rhythmic breathing and the lumps on the five beds, Ruby and Beatrice thought all the girls were sleeping. They startled when one girl suddenly sat up.

"Welcome to Hell," she croaked and fell back onto her bed.

Chapter Eight

RUBY AWAKENED TO A MUSTY smell. At first she felt disoriented. *Where am I?* She shivered when she tried to sit up. *My foot is killing me!* "Beatrice, can you look at my foot?"

"It looks infected, and I can feel heat with my hand held above it."

"What's wrong?" The girl on the bed next to Ruby sat up.

"She cut her foot on a sharp rock last night. We'll need to clean and dress it."

"I'll get Tom. He's in charge of medical."

I hate having him touch me, but I have no choice. "Okay."

Later, the girls were gathered around a rustic picnic table, but there were long narrow cushions on the benches. Cornmeal mush and milk was for breakfast that first morning. The three men sat nearby drinking coffee and eating eggs, ham, and toast with jelly.

Ruby looked around the all-purpose room. The ceiling was about nine feet high, and six small windows were positioned just below it. A colorful oriental rug was in the center of the room. Toward the wall to the right of the door were two treadle sewing machines and straight-back chairs and three rocking chairs.

The makeshift kitchen was on the right. There were shelves that held a variety of dishes and cookware, a sideboard held three wooden boxes for silverware, cooking utensils, and knives. A black sink with two compartments rested on four legs, and a wooden washtub with a crank wringer and an attached washboard occupied the space beside the sink. There was a black wood cook stove and an icebox.

Ruby asked the girl next to her, "Where's the bathroom?"

"I'll show you."

Hopping on one foot, Ruby followed her guide to the door. "I'll wait for you outside."

Ruby closed the door; the odor almost causing her to lose her breakfast. The chemical toilet was beside a wooden stand with a pitcher and bowl on the top and sliding doors below. Ruby opened the doors and was relieved to find shelves filled with hygiene necessities. An oblong galvanized tub about six feet long fit against the wall with only inches to spare.

When she returned, a meeting was called. Everyone was seated cross-legged on the rug.

Ruby was surprised that the guru was dressed in white. His shirt sleeves looked like wings when he held up his arms to signal the start. "You'll be Aster." He gestured toward Ruby. "Your name is Dahlia." He told Beatrice her new name while smiling and swinging his arms.

"Family, meet our new girls, Aster and Dahlia." Yuri introduced Begonia, Poppy, Hyacinth, Iris, and Heather. "We begin our days by meditating. Close your eyes and allow your minds to become blank. Everyone must join in or there will be consequences. Greet the Great Light. "Um-m-m-m…" Tom stood watching beside Yuri.

<u>The Devil comes as an angel of light to deceive</u>. Ruby closed her eyes and silently prayed to her Heavenly Father. *"I pray not only for strength and protection, but for your rescue and not only for Beatrice and me. Help us make it safely through this day."* Amen.

"Tom will assign your duties while I bring Aster and Dahlia to my room for a private conversation. He came over to the girls, grasped their hands, and lifted them to their feet. Five pairs of sympathetic eyes followed their retreat. Yuri knew about the injury and kept pace accordingly. His room was at one end of the house and Tom's and Guy's at the other.

The room was surprisingly elaborate, with a white canopied bed, thick wall-to-wall royal blue rug, and two velvet brocade upholstered chairs. Yuri gestured to the chairs. "You will both become my brides today, but we'll wait a few days before we come together and I infuse you with the light. Only when the vibrations of spiritual, mental, and emotional are harmonious will it be time for us to enjoy physical union. This afternoon we will conduct the weddings." He narrowed his yellow speckled brown eyes, "You will play nice, won't you?" His gaze was piercing as Ruby and Beatrice nodded. *I'll say that I don't at that sham wedding. In my mind…Oh Patrick!*

Chapter Nine

RUBY CLENCHED HER FISTS AND fought tears. Beatrice bent double and sobbed. The girls looked at the plain white shifts and wreaths of flowers on their beds. "Ruby, I think we have to do this. It would be dangerous not to." Beatrice was hiccupping after every other word spoken.

Ruby's arms encircled her friend. "Yuri is not licensed to perform weddings, so what will happen today is not legal. Poppy is tuning her violin, and we have only fifteen minutes to get ready. Jesus is here with us." Ruby pulled out tissues for both of them.

The girls stepped into an indoor spiral flower garden. All the housemates were positioned within the spiral. In the center, Yuri waited with his arms outstretched. The violin music filled the scented atmosphere with mournful tones. Ruby and Beatrice hesitated.

"Come, Dahlia and Aster, come to your spiritual bridegroom. Dahlia will be first."

Shaking, Beatrice stepped into the circle.

"Will you, Dahlia, obey Yuri at all times?"

Through tight lips Beatrice murmured, "I do."

"Will you take Yuri, your spiritual bridegroom, as your husband?"

Almost inaudible, a shaky whisper issued forth. "I do."

His flabby hand, shining with moisture, grabbed hers. Beatrice recoiled; his face reddened and his smile wavered. "Darling, it's my turn now. I, Yuri, promise to teach Dahlia how to please her husband. Obedience will be learned through suffering. I declare Dahlia is my wife from this day forward." Holding out his arms Yuri coaxed, "Come, Beautiful." He gave Beatrice a bear hug.

How awful for Beatrice. I can't move. God, give me strength. <u>I am your strength.</u> Ruby endured a similar indignity next, but the ceremony was decidedly more formal.

The special dinner entrée of surf and turf, haddock and steak, and side dishes of potatoes and mixed vegetables was served family style on a lace tablecloth. The girls ate in silence.

"Brides, gather around me and my two new brides." Yuri flung his flabby arms around their trembling slender shoulders. "We will now celebrate! Guy, bring it in!"

Guy pushed a large wooden cart covered with an assortment of alcohol and glasses as well as drugs and paraphernalia. *God, I need some guidance here.*

"May I go to the bedroom now? I need to get off this foot. May Dahlia go too to help me?" Ruby smiled sweetly and folded her hands.

Yuri scowled and mulled over his decision. He nodded, and the girls scooted out from under his possessive arms. Ruby gagged as she got a whiff of body odor.

Beatrice sat on the side of Ruby's bed; she carefully unwrapped the bandage and examined the foot. "It looks better. Let's leave the bandage off for a little while."

Before long they were both asleep although the party was noisy.

Chapter Ten

OVER THE NEXT TWO DAYS all the girls shared their stories with Ruby and Beatrice. Putting two and two together, Ruby explained, "All of us girls were kidnapped from islands only accessible by that seaplane. There is no telephone or electricity, so there is no address. None of these creeps own a car, so there is no identification to tell who these men really are or where they originated from. We girls have no way of contacting our families, and that's the way they want it. When they buy groceries, they always go to Garden Isle, never to the mainland."

Gay, aka Begonia, nodded vigorously. "This is a kind of hideout, but there must be a way for us to contact someone."

Natalie, aka Iris, jumped to her feet, "Wait a minute! I heard something last week coming from the storage room."

Grasping Natalie's arm, Eleanor, aka Hyacinth, shook Natalie as if to shake out the answer. "What did it sound like?"

"I'll try to describe what I heard…click, click. clickety, click."

Hyacinth thought a moment. "Could it be a CB radio? Maybe they're communicating…"

Ruby brightened. "It could be. My boyfriend showed me how to contact the CB on the ferry. If I could somehow get the key to the storage room, I could find the CB and let him know we're alive. There's no way anyone can find us here though." A collective sigh was the response to Ruby's proposed tactic.

"We need to join in some serious praying. Who's in?" Beatrice' and five girls' arms shot up immediately. "Before we leave this room in the morning, we'll pray."

Next morning, all seven girls knelt by their beds. Ruby prayed, "Heavenly Father, we come humbly before your throne. Would you please make an opportunity for us to unlock that storage room? Nothing is impossible with you. You are the same yesterday, today, and forever. As we kneel before you, we pray that every girl here will know your love and grace. You know how we all need your strength to endure one more day here. We pray for all of our families and friends. In Jesus' name we pray, Amen."

"Do you know the Lord's prayer? Let's pray it together." Sobs were interspersed as the familiar words were prayed.

With tear-stained face, Natalie whispered, "I believe the Lord will rescue all of us. Gay and I have been here the longest, six months already."

Ruby, who had never been a leader, looked lovingly at each girl. "We need to go now. Just remember this: "God loves each of you so much he can't take his eyes off you."

Chapter Eleven

Ruby sat at the sewing machine making linen shifts. Yuri had assigned her the tasks that could be done while sitting. The day before, she had washed laundry while sitting on a stool.

Guy and Tom sat on the carpet playing checkers nearby. Ruby suddenly caught sight of the key to the storage room that had noiselessly fallen out of Guy's pocket. *I need to pick that up without being noticed. Father, help me.* "I'll be right back. Nature calls!" In one motion, Ruby stood and swiped the key.

There was a kerosene lantern in the storage room that Ruby lit before closing the door. *Lord, where is that CB radio?* Over in the corner there was a square of fabric covering something. She pulled off the cloth. It was the radio! *Help me remember everything Patrick showed me.* <u>I am with you always.</u>

Ruby made contact with the ferry's radio. Patrick answered the signal. "Ruby and Beatrice are at GLK. Help. Over and out." *I can't dawdle.* Ruby opened the door a crack and made sure the coast was clear; she gently shut the door and went into the all-purpose room.

Before she returned to the sewing machine, Ruby bent down and abruptly stood up. "I think your key fell out of your pocket. Here it is."

"Thanky." Guy shoved the key in his pocket and moved a checker.

Beatrice, who was making egg salad sandwiches, saw everything and nodded.

Later, Ruby and Beatrice went into the bedroom. "Did you get through?"

"Yes, but I didn't have very much time to give the message. I said we are at GLK."

Beatrice groaned. "That's not very much to go on, Ruby! I know what you're going to say. That God will help them find us. There's not much time. Tomorrow night I'm being summoned, and the next night you will be." The pallor of her face, in deep contrast to her black hair, spoke volumes about her anxiety and fear.

Ruby reached out to her friend, hugged her gently, and said nothing. *What can I say?*

Chapter Twelve

"**I**'M SCARED TO GO BACK to sleep." Beatrice whispered.

"After that nightmare, I'd feel the same way." Ruby soothed her friend as she prayed silently. The girls went back to restless sleep.

At the first sign of dawn, Ruby rose and looked toward the all-purpose room. Tom and Yuri were talking. Ruby crept closer but kept out of sight.

"I didn't know we brought a preacher's kid until I saw the poster on the window of the general store." Tom was wringing his hands.

"You might have brought the wrath of Almighty God upon us! This could finish us." Yuri's carotid arteries pulsated.

"The other poster showed the picture of the store's daughter so that's why I didn't go in to get the groceries. We'll have to find a different island where we can shop undetected."

That sounds like they're running from something.

Later, while the girls ate cold, lumpy cream of wheat with no milk or sugar, Ruby glanced at Beatrice. Her eyes were bloodshot with dark purple rings underneath.

Yuri bellowed, "Leave that slop, and come to the carpet now!"

The guru's bulging eyes pierced each girl's as he scanned the circle. "This morning we're going to channel the dragon. Guy put on the visualization music." Weird music played on the old Victrola. "Close your eyes and bring up your dragon. No one may leave for any reason." Yuri pounded his fist on the carpet.

Ruby closed her eyes and prayed. *Oh Lord, you are the power of all that exists in the universe; you don't just have power. I know this. The dragon's power was broken when you defeated him. That happened when Jesus died on the cross. By Your help I know that we'll get out of here. Amen.*

After the meditation and teaching, Yuri dismissed everyone. "Get back to work!"

Events during the daytime were uneventful, but Ruby and Beatrice were dreading the evening events. Ruby kept trying to assure Beatrice. "Your Heavenly Father is with you."

Yuri and his men were in a foul mood all day and imbibed liberally.

Beatrice had gone to the guru's room, and the other girls had crawled into their beds when Ruby thought she heard a stick snap. She crept to the door and peered into the darkness.

"Ruby, Jeanne and I came to get you and Beatrice." Patrick whispered.

"I'll be right back." Ruby gently closed the door.

"Girls, come on now! We're being rescued!" All the girls whipped off the blankets, emptied the drawers, and tied belongings in the blankets.

"Put on your shoes quickly!" Ruby directed.

"What's going on?" Beatrice poked her head in the door.

"Hurry up! Come with us." Ruby glanced at Beatrice while tying her shoes. The girls gathered by the door. Beatrice ran to her bed and threw on her shoes not bothering to tie them. The escapees were so quiet in their exit that you could have heard a pin drop in the house.

They stepped into thick darkness. Patrick and Jeanne brought flashlights but didn't turn them on until the group could no longer see the house. Although the path between the rocks was narrow, they all moved as fast as possible. Natalie tripped over a protruding root and fell. Eleanor helped her get back up.

Finally, in the moonlight they saw the craggy shoreline and a cabin cruiser roped to a dock post. "Watch out for the shells, rocks and driftwood." Patrick cautioned.

A cool breeze blew the thin white dresses as the girls slogged across the littered sand. They looked like a company of angels. Blanche shivered, "My hands and feet are numb."

Jeanne encouraged, "It's just a little ways further. The cabin cruiser is heated and there were blankets."

Ruby stepped near her twin. "We brought our own clothes. Will there be room so we can change out of these?"

"Yes. You can go into the head, the dining room, or the berth. Patrick will have his back turned at the helm so you'll all have privacy."

"We're sailing to the lighthouse to dock the boat. After that, we'll walk over the bridge to my truck, and from there, I'll drive you to the Miller's house. I think you'll probably spend the night there and tomorrow you can go home to your families. Don't worry. Even though we didn't know we were getting you five girls, we're thrilled that we got to rescue you too." Patrick leaned over resting his hands on his knees.

Jeanne stood to the side of the boat. "Watch your step" was repeated as each girl embarked.

Patrick stood beside Ruby, "After you're changed could you sit by me?"

Ruby was a bit disoriented with all that had happened. She nodded gravely. Glancing toward heaven and folding her hands in the prayer position, Ruby prayed, "Thank you, Father. Thank you for Patrick and Jeanne who had the courage to come to get us. Help each girl as she reconnects with her family. In Jesus' name, Amen."

Chapter Thirteen

WHEN THE TRUCK DROVE TOWARD the Miller home, Patrick had to keep from hitting any of the vehicles lining the street. He couldn't drive into the driveway. "We'll have to park over on Maple Street and walk to your house."

"Okay. I'll go tell the girls." Ruby got out and went to the truck bed where they were packed like sardines. "We'll have to walk to our house. It's not too far."

Jeanne stood by the tailgate. "We'll be glad to walk and stretch our cramped legs."

Ruby and Jeanne led the way to their front door and rang the bell. Their mother answered. They rushed into her arms. When the twins looked inside, they saw that the living room and dining room were filled with people kneeling, sitting, and standing. The community had gathered to pray for the safe return of Ruby, Jeanne, Beatrice, and Patrick. Charlie with Patrick's parents squirmed through the crowd and enveloped their children.

Cynthia was the first to notice the shivering girls who had stepped away from the door. She went toward them; Ruby noticed and joined her mother. "Mama, these girls were with me, and we all escaped together." Cynthia's hand flew to her mouth.

"Come inside out of this cold. We can get acquainted later."

As the girls entered, the guests exited. Pastor Nate stood beside the door thanking them for coming to pray. Patrick spoke to Ruby. "I'll talk to you tomorrow and see you Sunday."

Ari, Elizabeth, Marty, and Lizzy greeted the twins. Lizzy asked, "Monday Marty and I would like to come see you. Is that too soon?"

Ruby nodded. "You'd be welcome."

Charlie interrupted and shook hands with Patrick and Jeanne. "You have my deepest gratitude." Beatrice hugged Patrick and the twins. "Ruby, I'll call you tomorrow," she said.

Ruby and Jeanne closed the door and looked at each other. "Talk later?" They laughed. "Yep, we're in sync again."

Their mother was ladling bowls of clam corn chowder. "My sweet babies, I love you."

Ruby was overcome with the emotion filling her throat. "Oh Mama…"

Cynthia wiped her tears on the hem of her apron, "Girls, could you please bring these into the dining room? I'll get these biscuits into the baskets. I already brought in the pitcher of ice water and glasses."

When Ruby passed out the bowls, she noticed the girls looked bewildered. "What are you worried about?"

Blanche answered, "We have to call our parents."

Nathan, with deep concern in his eyes, looked at each girl, "You may use our phone whenever you're ready."

Ruby stood behind her father resting her palms on his shoulders. "Mama said you are welcome to spend as much time here as you'll need. Jeanne and I have pjs you can all wear. Why don't we enjoy this while it's hot?"

Nathan called Cynthia and Jeanne to join them. "Heavenly Father, Thank you for all you did to bring all the girls here safe and sound. Thank you for this food. In Jesus' name. Amen."

He looked up. "My wife and I ate earlier, but we'll join you for dessert and coffee later."

"Enjoy, girls. There's more where that came from." Cynthia's smiled warmly. During the meal, she used her to-do pad to take notes that were helpful to the weekend plans. "After your tummies are filled, why don't you all go up and get ready for bed. I'll call your parents and let them know you're safe here. They will have directions so they can come to get you. What do you think girls?"

The girls nodded and lined up by Cynthia's chair. Cynthia wrote:

Blanche Edwards, aka Poppy, Long Island (Portland), Saturday

Gaynor Johnson, aka Begonia, Cliff Island (Portland), Saturday

Sadie Lawrence, aka Hyacinth North Haven (Rockland), Saturday?

Eleanor Campbell, aka Daisy, Swan Island (Bar Harbor), Sunday

Natalie Smith, aka Iris, Deer Isle (Ellsworth), Saturday

She also jotted down their telephone numbers.

For dessert Jeanne brought out small brownie sundaes and hot chocolate with marshmallows. Before following the twins upstairs, the girls thanked their hosts.

Ruby hesitated at the foot of the stairs hearing her father talking. "Yes, Constable Perry. All the girls who have been missing are here. They were all kidnapped and taken to a remote place in Gulls Harbor. Patrick O'Connor and our daughter, Jeanne, rescued them. Ruby alerted Patrick on the ferry's CB and helped the other six escape. The captors probably are still in the house." There was a minute or so of silence. "Yes, I can put Ruby on the phone." He glanced toward the stairs. "She'll be with you in a minute."

Ruby told the constable everything and gave directions. "Please let the girls know we'll bring those creeps in. Even though you don't know who they are, we'll investigate. We'll speak with you girls when you're comfortable. Tell your parents I'll come by in the late morning. Good night, Miss Miller"

"Good night, Sir."

She hung up and ascended the stairs. Her parents were watching "I Love Lucy." *This must be hard for them to imagine what I've been through.*

Chapter Fourteen

JEANNE HAD TAKEN CHARGE OF the bedtime rituals. One-by-one the girls washed up. Fortunately, the Millers had stockpiled tooth brushes. The girls hadn't brushed their teeth in captivity, just rinsing with water after meals. Depending on the sizes, the twins shared their pajamas. Natalie wrapped her arms around herself. "This feels so soft and comfy. Thank you."

Between the double bed and three cots, there was ample room for the five girls in Jeanne's bedroom. Jeanne and Ruby went into Ruby's room and shut the door quietly. The first thing the womb mates did was to hold each other and pour out the tears they'd held back. They wanted to find out so many things from each other, but they fell onto the bed exhausted still holding on tightly. The light was shining from the bedside table.

At 2:00 they suddenly awakened. Silently, they undressed and slipped on some pajamas. Jeanne raised the window; a cool breeze refreshed the room. "Do you want to talk about it, Ruby? This may be our best chance with everything going on."

"Yes." Ruby reached for her twin's hand. "How did you and Patrick find us?"

"I'll start at the beginning. When you and Beatrice didn't return, Lizzy and I knew something must be up. For the next few days, the whole community was alerted that you two were missing and a search party went out. We put posters around the island, in the ferry, and around Covington. All of us were praying. I was a basket case and felt like half of me was missing. The ache was unbearable until Patrick got your message." Jeanne left on tiptoe to get some water from the bathroom.

"What happened after that?" Ruby grasped her knees and listened intently.

"Patrick and I got together to decide what to do. We had no idea what GLK meant. Both of us knew we wouldn't rest until we found out. When you said, "Help", we knew we needed to act fast. Yesterday we called our bosses that we wouldn't be in to work for a couple of days. We hightailed it to Simpson's Library; when the doors opened, we began to research. After two hours of finding nothing, the librarian came over. I told her about your message.

Near closing, she said it was a long shot, but she remembered a custody case where the wife had concerns about a cult.

Ruby sat up straight. "That is an answer to our prayers. It is a cult."

Jeanne continued. "Mrs. Simpson found the article in the *Bangor Daily News* micro phish. We were so glad that the article revealed that it was in Gulls Harbor. But where it was located we didn't have a clue. Today, we decided to go see Otis Moore, but no one knew anything about our plans. They would have tried to stop us. Mr. Moore spent time describing where he thought the Great Light Kingdom could be. He had docked once at Gulls

Harbor and had seen a Native long house. And he told us about the dangers of the rough terrain. Patrick and I were scared, yes, but we wanted to try to rescue you and Beatrice. Knowing Patrick had navigational experience, Mr. Moore offered his cabin cruiser. You know the rest."

"I do want to share with you, Jeanne, but it's still so fresh. I love you so much." *What would I do without my twin? She showed so much courage.*

"I love you so much! You can let me know when we can talk again. I can't imagine…" Jeanne's cheeks, neck, and pajama top were soaked with tears.

Chapter Fifteen

*E*MOTIONS WERE HEIGHTENED THE MORNING after the rescue. All the girls had called their parents, Patrick had called Ruby, and Ruby had called Beatrice who had come to the Millers' when she'd hung up since she didn't want to be alone with her father working.

Everyone startled at the sound of the brass knocker. Nathan found Constable Perry at the door anxious to call a meeting. "Please call everyone together. I need to explain the events of the morning."

"I will, Constable Perry. Shall we gather in the living room?"

When everyone was comfortable, Nathan asked to pray. He led the group in the Lord's Prayer. "The Lord said He would never, ever forsake His children. This is Constable Perry; he's here to tell us some news. Please tell him your names and where your home is."

"I called police in Covington, and a squadron of four met me in the office within an hour. After discussing the situation, we decided to go out to Gulls Harbor immediately. We thought chances were good that the suspects were sleeping and didn't even know of the escape. We boarded the seaplane and sailed at a high speed to the destination." The constable cleared his throat.

"Would you like a cup of coffee?" offered Cynthia.
"Please."

Sipping the hot brew, he continued. "We approached the house undetected and found the door unlocked. The three suspects were sleeping when we arrived, but not for long. We law enforcement surprised them. Two are on their way to Thomaston Prison. Thomas Collins and Raymond Merrill had escaped from there last fall."

Eyes popped and mouths flew open. "Do you-u me-ean Gay and I were held by escaped convicts for six months?" Natalie was shaking uncontrollably.

"What about Yuri?" asked Ruby.

"Horace Clark is presently under armed guard at Southern Maine Medical Center. There was a scuffle with us, and he got injured. A police helicopter flew him for medical attention. From there, he'll join his buddies at Thomaston. He had served his sentence, made a fair amount of money selling illegal things. He found the abandoned long house and furnished it. Later, he bought a flying boat. He studied the Source and adapted some of Father Yod's philosophies and practices, but he combined that with the evil and twisted thinking of an ex-convict. He began to call himself Yuri, the Earthly Spiritual Father. When he visited the other two in prison, he described where he lived. So they found him after their escape.

You girls will be asked to witness to what happened there. Right now, go home to your families and resume your lives. I recommend that you rest for a few days and eat well to regain the muscle mass you've lost from the malnutrition. When you're ready, you may want to go to see counselors who have dealt with traumas of kidnapping and sex trafficking. Any police precinct should have referrals for that."

Beatrice stood abruptly, went to the constable, and reached out her hand. All the other girls gathered around to shake his hand. "Thank you, Mr. Perry, and please thank the other policemen. Now we know those creeps won't be around to try to find us." Ruby spoke for all of them knowing that that was their greatest fear. *Thank you, Jesus! You saved us!*

"I'm just glad that those scallywags will be locked up for a long time." He turned toward Nathan and Cynthia. "Would you please record the parents' names, addresses and phone numbers and bring them to the office?"

"My wife will do that. Thank you, Sir."

"You're most welcome. I'm just doing my job. Good day." He waved to the girls.

Chapter Sixteen

"How would you like to have homemade pizzas for lunch?" Cynthia didn't wait for an answer when all the girls smiled.

Gay asked, "What can I do to help, Mrs. Miller?"

"You may all call me Cynthia. I'll make enough dough for four large pizzas. Ruby and Jeanne can set you up with the vegetables to cut. I'll have the dough made in a jiffy."

Each pizza ended up being a culinary masterpiece. While everyone was savoring each tasty morsel, there was a knock on the door. Cynthia rose and opened the door.

"Do we have the right place? My wife and I are here to get our daughter."

"What is her name?"

"Sadie Lawrence."

"Yes, she's with us. Please come in. I'm Cynthia Miller. Sadie called you from here this morning. I'll go get her."

Cynthia came back with Sadie. "Daddy you came too! You always golf on Saturdays."

"Oh, Sadie!" Nothing more was said as Sadie found comfort in her parents' arms.

"Please join us for lunch in the dining room. Just follow us."

"Thank you." Ruth Lawrence wiped her tears on the Kleenex Sadie offered.

Ruby and Jeanne brought two chairs from the kitchen, and Cynthia laid out place settings.

"Help yourselves." Nathan gestured toward the two remaining pizzas and lemonade.

Sadie introduced her parents. Her friends were overjoyed that Sadie was going home but were sad because they'd miss her. Sniffles went around the table.

"Who would like strawberry shortcake and root beer? I'll serve it outside on the patio."

Jeanne glanced toward the street. "A car is driving in. It's a blue Packard."

"That's my parents." Blanche's lip trembled.

Cynthia put her arm around the thin shoulders. "I'll go with you, Honey." They hadn't reached the car when both doors were flung open and Blanche's parents ran to their daughter.

"Blanchie. Oh, my girl." Her mother reached her first and held Blanche against her ample bosom. Then, her father wrapped his long muscular arms around them both in a tearful family reunion.

Cynthia looked on until they had pulled apart. "Please come join us in the backyard for some strawberry shortcake and root beer."

"We can do that, but we can't stay very long. The ferry is scheduled to leave here at 2:00, and then we'll need to catch the 5:30 one to Long Island."

Ruby and Blanche promised to never forget each other. "Come upstairs with me."

Blanche leaned over toward her parents. "I'm going inside for a few minutes. I'll be right out."

Upon entering her bedroom, Ruby smiled and pointed. "You can have any doll you like. Which one do you choose?"

Blanche chose a dark haired beauty wearing a riding habit. "She will remind me to pray for you. Thanks, Ruby for helping me know about Jesus. I love you."

A shiny, deep blue Buick convertible slowed and parked in the driveway. When Ruby and Blanche crossed the porch, they saw a tall blonde wearing sunglasses and a head covering. She untied the kerchief, folded it, and slipped it into the glove compartment. Afterward, she glanced in the rearview mirror and tucked a few errant wisps into place. When her legs emerged, her flawless pedicure peeked out from leather sandals. She wore a red collared blouse tucked into a plaid pleated skirt. Seeing the girls, she lowered her sunglasses and called out. "Is Gaynor Johnson here?"

"Yes, she's in the backyard, Mrs. Johnson. We're going there now. Gay will be so glad to see you!"

On the patio Blanche stood with her parents after hugging everyone. "We can never repay your kindness." Her father shook hands with Nathan and Cynthia.

Gay and her mother embraced, and the Millers introduced themselves to Bridgett Johnson. "Gaynor, I made reservations at the Seaside Inn for tonight. Turning toward the Millers and reaching out her hand she said, "Thank you for all you did for my daughter. Can you direct me to the Seaside Inn?"

Cynthia wrote the directions on her pad. "Can I interest you in some soda?"

"Thank you, but I'll pass. Gaynor, say your good byes now so we can be on our way."

Chapter Seventeen

"Let's go in and start supper." Cynthia put an arm around each twin. "The Swains will be rolling in about an hour from now."

"We can make salad if that will help." Ruby offered.

"Yes, and it's wonderful to be here in the kitchen together again."

Jeanne put a stack of records on the record player. While they worked they sang different parts along with the vocalist who was singing: *Put your Hand in the Hand.*

Put your hand in the hand of the Man who stilled the waters. (stilled the waters)

Put your hand in the hand of the Man who calmed the sea. (calmed the sea)

Take a look at yourself, and you can look at others differently.

By putting your hand in the hand of the Man from Galilee. (Man from Galilee)

They joined hands and swung around in the kitchen laughing. Just then a couple came through the door holding hands. The man was dressed in a plaid shirt and dark brown pants held up with button and loop suspenders. His hat was dilapidated but he held it in his hand politely. The woman with him looked almost exactly like Natalie, with the same light brown hair and blue eyes.

"Your husband said we could come in to ask you for a drink. "We're Uzziah and Lula Smith."

Cynthia introduced herself and the twins. "It's nice to meet you. Would you like lemonade, soda, or water?"

"Lemonade please," answered Lula.

We've come to fetch our dottah. Jake's my brothah, and Alice is cookin' us some vittles fo suppah. We tootled over on my fishin' boat, docked it, and walked up heah." Uzziah Smith bent to catch his breath.

Jeanne and Ruby nodded and headed outside. They met up with Natalie over by the outdoor fireplace. "You live close enough that we can visit." Ruby grinned with pleasure at the thought.

"As often as I can for sure. We'll probably leave pretty soon to go to my aunt and uncle's for a fish fry and rhubarb cobbler. They asked us to spend the night."

Jeanne smiled. "Your parents seem pretty tired. I'll ask if Daddy can drive you there,"

Nathan came over wearing his barbeque sauce-splashed apron. "Good idea! They're still inside so I'll offer when they come out." He went back to the grilling.

Cynthia and the parents entered the patio area. "You ready, girl?"

"Yes, I am Daddy. I'm lookin' forward to seein' Uncle Jake and Aunt Alice."

"Natalie, wait for a minute." Jeanne went to her room and came out promptly.

"That is beautiful." Natalie stared at a foot long model ship.

"I want you to have it."

"Did you make this? It was a lot of work." Natalie turned the ship in every angle.

"Yes, I made it, Natalie. It will be a blessing for you to accept it."

"Thank you, Jeanne."

My twin has a kind and generous nature.

"We'll see that she comes to visit some weekend. No words can express how thankful we are for you brave girls." Lula hugged the twins, and Uzziah whisked off his hat with a flourish and bowed.

Cynthia took over grilling the barbequed chicken and corn on the cob. Nathan helped Natalie and Lula get in the VW's back seat. Then, he and Uzziah hopped in the front. Uzziah stuck his hat out the window and waved it until the car disappeared from view.

Eleanor stuck her head out the back door. "I fell asleep. Is there anything I can do to help? They've all left but me. Mom called to tell me my family will arrive tomorrow around three. I'd like to join you for church in the morning."

Ruby took two steps at a time. "Come on, Ellie, we can set the table in the dining room. Mama said to use the best dishes and silver. I already put on the lace tablecloth and picked some flowers to put in her favorite vase. We want everything to be nice for the visiting pastor, Rev. Swain."

As the girls worked, they made plans. "You can bunk with me tonight," offered Ruby.

It may be awhile until I can sleep again in my room by myself. Maybe Jeanne and I can share her room for awhile...

Chapter Eighteen

"We brought a sweet potato pie and a pot of collard greens." Corinne Swain came into the kitchen holding out the dishes.

"Thank you, Mrs. Swain. I'm Ruby and my friend here is Ellie. We'll serve supper in a jiffy." Their guest left the house and joined her husband on the patio.

"She's such a beautiful lady. Her face glows. Did you ever see such long lashes and not a bit of mascara?" Ruby brought the potato salad to the table.

"I love her dress with the irises all along the bottom." Eleanor tossed the salad and carried it into the dining room.

"Mama said she sings like Mahalia Jackson. I can't wait to hear her solo tomorrow."

Ruby's mouth watered from the sweet smell of corn roasted to a golden brown followed by the spicy fragrance of barbequed chicken as Nathan held the door open for Cynthia and Jeanne bringing in the grilled food. After the platters had been placed on the table, Ruby retrieved the biscuits from the warm oven, placed them in a cloth-lined basket, and laid it on the table beside the tub of butter.

Ebenezer held the door for his wife. He wore a gray blazer, navy blue pants, and a white shirt and multi-colored tie. "Welcome to our home, but first things first.

Be comfortable, brother. You may hang your jacket and tie up here in the hall," Instructed Nathan.

Family and guests sat at the table. "We'd be honored for you to bless the food before it gets cold." Nathan tapped his friend's shoulder.

During supper, conversation turned toward recent events. Ebenezer glanced around the table and addressed Nathan. "We're glad we could come this Sunday after everything you have all endured this past week. You can relax while I preach. This evening may I use your office to pray and go over my notes?"

"That will be hunky dory. I'll take you there after we have coffee and eat that amazing pie Corinne baked for us." Nathan smiled the widest Ruby had seen since she'd come home.

Ebenezer Swain is just the person Daddy needed. Lord, what timing...

The men left for the office, and the girls cleaned the kitchen.

"May I play the piano and practice the solo for tomorrow?" asked Corinne.

"Of course, but only if we can come in and be your audience." Cynthia smiled and hooked her arm in Corinne's, and led her into the living room.

"I thought I would sing *God Will Take Care of You*. Please wait just a minute while I get out the sheet music." Corinne sang with strength of spirit.

> Be not dismayed whate'er betide. (God will take care of you.)

Beneath His wings of love abide. (God will take
    care of you.)
Through days of toil when heart does fail.
When dangers fierce your path assail,

God will take care of you,
Through every day,
All of the way,
God will take care of you; He will take care of you.

Corinne sang the rest of the song and then motioned for everyone to gather around the piano. For the next hour they sang familiar Gospel songs. *I feel a little more like myself now.*

Chapter Nineteen

*T*o say that Ruby hadn't slept well is an understatement. The bedroom was still dark. *That nightmare I keep having…I hope Ellie slept better than I did.* "A-R-R-R!" Ruby sprang up like a jack-in-the-box. Eleanor was thrashing and screaming.

Ruby reached over and touched her friend's shoulder. "You're safe, Ellie."

Eleanor, shaking violently, opened her eyes. "I was dreaming about…Oh, I can never tell anyone what he made me do!"

Alarmed, Ruby rushed to her parents' room. She gently touched her mother. "Mama, please come to my room. It's Ellie." Ruby was careful to whisper close to Cynthia's ear.

"I'll come." Cynthia whispered as she slipped on her robe.

When they walked through the door, Eleanor's eyes were shut tight, and she was standing like a wraith in the middle of the room. The bedding was askew, and feathers floated through the air. Cynthia went to her and followed protocol for dealing with a sleepwalker. She came to stand beside Eleanor and gently turned her and helped her sit in the chair. "Sweetie, let's not try to shake her awake. We'll remake the bed, get a fresh pillow, and settle her back in."

Settling in beside her friend, Ruby hugged her mother. "Thanks, Mama, for helping."

"I'll see you in the morning." Cynthia kissed her daughter and carefully closed the door.

Thunder rumbled in the distance and lightning flashed through the curtains waking Ruby. Eleanor was sleeping peacefully. *Heavenly Father, I thank you for another day even though it's going to pour.(smile) Please help my friends and their families...*<u>I make all the crooked places straight.</u>

Both girls were awake. "I want to go to church, but I don't have anything to wear."

"You're about Jeanne's size. I'm sure she has something for you."

Jeanne, dressed in a golden yellow maxi dress, knocked on the door. "Can I come in? I brought something I thought you might like to wear to church." She held out a pale blue midi dress with a collar, puff sleeves, and an attached belt that tied in the back.

"Are you sure? This is a beautiful dress." Eleanor's hand flew to her mouth.

"Try it on, Silly." The fit was perfect, and the shade of blue perfectly matched her eyes.

Ruby pulled on a mint green midi dress. The girls fixed each other's hair.

As they left the bedroom, the rain looked like tears streaming down the windows.

The smell of fresh brew wafted up the stairs as the girls descended. The women were in the kitchen wearing aprons over their church clothes. "Good morning, girls. You look lovely."

Cynthia waved toward the dining room. "We'll eat in there. Would you please set the table?"

The family and their guests made quick work of the breakfast of homemade waffles, scrambled eggs, and ham. Nathan stood, "Shall we go? I think we have enough umbrellas for all of us. It's raining cats and dogs. Ayuh." Cynthia and the girls shrugged into their coats.

"We'll follow you." Ebenezer helped Corinne into her coat and reached for his blazer and tie. "What a gully washer!" Holding the umbrellas they all ran to the cars. The car tires sprayed rain water all the way to Seacrest Chapel.

Casey (affectionately known as Bubba) and his wife Dorothy were standing inside the church door. When he handed out the bulletins his jowls jiggled. "Welcome to the house of the Lord." First, Dorothy met Corinne; then she smiled and hugged the women and girls.

Pastor Nate introduced his friend. "This is Pastor Ebenezer. God uses him to bless your socks off."

The men shook hands, and Casey and Dorothy parted to let the group pass. Dorothy tapped Ruby's shoulder. "I'm a piano teacher if you'd like some lessons. Your schedule, no charge."

Ruby's eyes sparkled. "I would love to do lessons."

Chapter Twenty

Following the break after the Sunday School closing exercises, the pastors and their wives sat together on the front pew, but the twins and Eleanor found seats together nearer the back. *I feel relieved not to be playing the piano today.* Ruby had found out that Dorothy rehearsed twice with the band.

"We want to thank our Father in Heaven for the safe return of our children. He took care of all four of them." Pastor Nate opened the service with that heartfelt prayer which evoked the sounds of sniffles and noses being blown.

With the very first worship song, the presence of the Lord filled the chapel. The congregation was encouraged to sing accompanied by the enthusiastic band. They sang:

> I will enter his gates with thanksgiving in my heart.
> I will enter his courts with praise.
> I will say this is the day the Lord has made.
> I will rejoice for he has made me glad…

Dorothy spoke from the piano. "That song came from the Maranatha singers and is taken from Psalm 100. Brother Smith will read that Psalm." Brian opened his Bible and read the beloved words of the Psalm:

> 1. Make a Joyful noise unto the LORD, all ye lands.

2. Serve the LORD with gladness; come before his presence with singing.
3. Know ye that the LORD he is God; it is he that hath made us and not we ourselves; we are his people, and the sheep of his pasture.
4. Enter into his gates with thanksgiving, and into his courts with praise; be thankful unto him, and bless his name.
5. For the LORD is good; his mercy is everlasting; and his truth endureth to all generations. Brian returned to the pew.

Following two hymns, announcements, and offering, Pastor Nate came to the pulpit as the worship band were leaving the platform. "Seacrest Chapel is blessed today with the ministry of Pastor Ebenezer Swain and his wife, Corinne. These saints of God have become very dear to our family. I first met Pastor Ebenezer at his church in Portland. His church had hosted twenty pastoral couples paying all of our hotel and meal expenses. When we were there, I asked him to come this Sunday to minister." A clap of thunder rattled the windows. "I guess the Lord Himself is agreeing."

He took time to look each congregant in the eyes. "Remember the account in Acts 8:26-40 where Philip, the deacon, is sent by God to the treasurer of the Queen of Ethiopia? He met up with the man sitting in a chariot reading from Isaiah 53:7-8. That man of distinction, an intelligent, accomplished black man, was the first recorded Gentile to become a believer in Jesus after the outpouring on Pentecost." He glanced at the piano. "Sister Corinne, please come and bless us with your solo."

It wasn't customary to clap after a solo, but the people stood together and clapped and clapped. Corinne blushed. "Thank y'all. Let that applause be lifted to the Lord."

Together the pastors stepped onto the platform. Nathan spoke, "We've been learning about the I ams of Christ. Today, Pastor Ebenezer is preaching about the Good Shepherd and His sheep." The men shook hands, and Pastor Nate settled beside Cynthia to listen.

"Corinne and I are privileged to be here this rainy morning." Glancing out the window he backtracked. "I goofed up. It isn't raining now." Attempts were made to stifle chuckles and giggles. Violet Moore sat with lips tight and arms folded.

"Please turn in your Bibles to Psalm 23. A little girl repeating the twenty-third psalm said it this way, 'The Lord is my shepherd, that's all I want.' (From the mouths of babes!)"

> "When I read the text, I'll add commentary from an anonymous writer."
> The Lord is my Shepherd-*That's Relationship!*
> I shall not want-*That's Supply!*
> He maketh me to lie down in green pastures-*That's Rest!*
> He leadeth me beside the still waters-*That's Refreshment!*
> He restoreth my soul-*That's Healing!*

He leadeth me in the paths of righteousness-*That's Guidance!*

For His name sake-*That's Purpose!*

Yea, though I walk through the valley of the shadow of death-*That's Testing!*

I will fear no evil-*That's Protection!*

For Thou art with me-*That's Faithfulness!*

Thy rod and Thy staff they comfort me-*That's Discipline!*

Thou preparest a table before me in the presence of mine enemies-*That's Hope!*

Thou annointest my head with oil-*That's Consecration!*

My cup runneth over-*That's Abundance!*

Surely goodness and mercy shall follow me all the days of my life-*That's Blessing!*

And I will dwell in the house of the Lord-*That's Security!*

Forever-*That's Eternity!* (KJV) Anonymous

"This morning's message is entitled *The Good Shepherd and the Naughty Sheep.*" Pastor Ebenezer first highlighted Jesus' message from John 10:1-18 Jesus is *the Good Shepherd* from John 10:14 where He plainly stated, 'I am the Good Shepherd.' He spoke at length from Luke 15:3-7 where Jesus told a parable that showed how much He cares about each person. *I see how He was my personal shepherd even at Great Light Kingdom.*

"*The naughty sheep* describes all of us. Earlier, Pastor Nate shared that the Ethiopian was reading Scripture from Isaiah 53. Verse 6 says, 'All we like sheep have gone astray; we have turned everyone to his own way…'" Why is God depicted as a shepherd and humans as sheep? The reason is because God behaves like a caring shepherd toward people who act like sheep needing his love and guidance before getting themselves in deep trouble." Ebenezer gulped some water.

"To show you what I mean, say if one of the sheep trots off the side of a cliff, all the others will follow. Haven't we often seen how people can be influenced by someone else to start taking drugs, engage in free love, follow misguided gurus, and make many unhealthy or even dangerous choices? We need the Good Shepherd every day."

"The message will conclude with a warning from Ezekiel 34:17-18. In this hour of unrest and uncertainty, the Lord's sheep must unselfishly care for each other. In context, this chapter was written to the shepherds and sheep of Israel, but it applies to us here today. 'As for you, my flock, thus says the Lord God; Behold I judge between sheep and sheep, between rams and male goats. Is it not enough for you to feed on the good pasture, that you must tread down with your feet the rest of your pasture; and to drink of clear water, that you must muddy the rest of the water with your feet?'"

Pastor Ebenezer closed his well-worn Bible after folding and inserting his notes. "Pastor, may I have liberty to appeal to your congregation?"

"Take your liberty, Pastor. I trust that our Lord is guiding your thoughts and words."

"Dear Brothers and Sisters, It's time for us to ask God to examine our motives and actions. Are you a naughty sheep making life difficult for others with your prejudices, abuses, complaints, and downright nastiness? Jesus is your Good Shepherd and will forgive you. He will help you bite your tongue if you'll stop before you say something you'll regret." The Word tells us that words are powerful and can cause great damage. Who here needs to think before you speak? Thank you for your kind attention. Thank you, Pastor Nate, for inviting me to share your pulpit."

Shoulders in front of Ruby began to shake. *That's Violet Moore if I live and breathe.* Pastor Nate, Pastor Ebenezer, and Brian Smith, joined by their wives, lined up in front of the altar rail. They prayed with community leaders, fishermen, teenagers, children, and Violet Moore. The band played softly as hearts were softened on Garden Isle, Maine.

Epilogue

Jeanne Ruth Miller

July, 1973

I thought I would starve that Sunday. We got home at 1:30! I held out my hand to my mother for the house key, she laid it in my palm, and I ran to the back. When I opened the door, I stood for a moment in disbelief. Running to the front door, I flung it open. "Come quick!"

"What's the matter?" Daddy asked, concern etched on his brow.

I couldn't answer, just pointed toward the kitchen. Car doors slammed as everyone ran into the house. They followed me to the back hallway. The seagull looked so pathetic lying stretched out on a bed of glass shards. Worse, it was not moving.

Corinne moved over to the bird. "I'm a vet tech. Let's see what we can do to help God's creature. It looks like it got disoriented in the thunder storm and broke through the window. First, I'll need to get this bird off the glass and onto a table."

Ruby ran upstairs to get an old towel. Mama stripped the oil cloth from a patio table and spread out the towel. Corinne carried the seagull and gently laid it down. She looked at the worried faces. "Good news. There doesn't seem to be any broken bones or wings. Some lacerations are deeper than others. It conked its head pretty hard. May I see what I can do?"

"Take your time. We'll get lunch. Girls, please come and help fill these skewers. When I first got up, I cut the veggies, shrimp, and steak tips. Your father is firing up the grill." We all pitched in but kept looking out. Finally, a wing fluttered and a throat quivered.

"Cynthia, would you mind if our feathered friend finds comfort in our laundry basket?" Daddy, wearing his apron, grabbed the broom and dust pan. "I went down cellar and got the basket." *All creatures great and small, all things wise and wonderful, the Lord God made them all… Little Seagully, here comes your bed.*

"If you have cardboard or plywood, I'd be glad to fix the window." Daddy got Pastor Ebenezer what he needed.

We were all busy beavers until we plopped our behinds onto the plastic chairs to eat our lunch. That's when the phone began ringing. I counted. It rang five times during lunch. Mama motioned to me to answer it.

It was the best phone call ever! I ran to Daddy. "Marty and Patrick asked Ruby and me on a date next Friday. They want to take us to a Dottie Rambo concert in Portland at the University of Southern Maine."

Yes. However, you wouldn't be able to get back home. The ferry…"

Pastor Ebenezer leaned over and whispered to Corinne, then, he spoke to Daddy. "They are welcome to spend the night with us. We're going, and they could follow us home after." Ruby was listening to the whole thing and nodded that she wanted to go.

I was excited and ran back in to tell Marty. After I talked to him, I was headed out the door and… b-r-ring! the phone rang again. It was Ellie's parents saying they were calling from a phone booth in Covington and that the ferry would arrive on Garden Isle in an hour. I made it to the top step when I heard the phone again and answered.

"Pastor, the call's for you." I came back to my plate of almost-cold food.

The Swains left quickly for an emergency. We decided that the smelts we had in the refrigerator would feed Barney. We agreed on that name after Corinne told us that the seagull was a male.

The Campbells came and drove Ellie home. They invited our whole family to come to Swan Island for a weekend. It's near Acadia National Park, Bar Harbor. *WOW…that would be sooo groovy.* It was only our family gathered around the supper table late that evening. We just looked from one to the other. What could we say?

Ruby Jane Miller

August, 1973

You're invited to take a walk along the beach with me. I'll tell you what has happened in the past three weeks. Jeanne left it up to me since I tend to be more detailed.

I know you're wondering about Barney. Good news! He improved more and more each day in the laundry basket on the back porch. I especially liked to watch how he ate the smelts in one big gulp. After four days, he tested both wings while Jeanne and I looked on. He turned his head toward us as if to say thank you and good bye; then he flew straight up from the basket.

Thursday, before the beach meeting, Marty and Lizzy were baptized. They stepped into the water holding hands. Twelve others were baptized. I was tearing up as Patrick strummed the hit song, *Through it All*, on his guitar. It seemed like all the people who lived on the island were on the shore including Ari and Elizabeth Ruben. Marty and Lizzy's mother came in the morning and went home Friday. Later, Lizzy told us how close mother and daughter became those two days.

The double date Friday exceeded all my expectations. Patrick treated me like a queen the whole time. He told me that he and his mother had been going to the Aquarius Oasis for "Kids are Special" meetings. When I feel more recovered, I'll join them. We ate at a French restaurant.

Then, we drove to Dottie Rambo's, *It's the Soul of Me*, concert that included some of my favorites she'd written.

The Swains were perfect hosts, but I'm afraid we kept them up way past their bedtime. Jeanne and I were both surprised when Marty and Patrick shared their calls for ministry. They told Pastor Swain their dreams and visions for Bible college and the Lord's work. We looked at each other, and Jeanne whispered, "It figures."

I responded, "It just goes to show…You never know what's going to happen next."

From the first day, the next week was a flurry of activities. A phone call from the governor's office turned out to be an invitation to come to the Maine State House. The press was invited to witness awards being given to Patrick, Jeanne, and me. From phone calls we found out the other families also had received invitations and that they were all going to attend.

I am bubbling over with excitement. Our family went to Augusta Wednesday morning; we spent the day touring the capital, the museum, and Fort Western, and we spent the night at the Best Western Hotel. Thursday morning, we showered and dressed in our brand new clothes and parked at the Maine State House. It was a life-changing experience! The conference room was packed with the girls and their families, and newspaper and television reporters; the governor, the attorney general, and Constable Perry sat facing the audience.

The room was elegant, lit by chandeliers, and the Maine flag and the American flag stood on pedestals in front. Constable Perry told the story of the rescue and said he was proud of the way we'd handled things. You know how shy I am, so you won't be surprised when I tell you that my knees shook like crazy when Patrick, Jeanne, and I were called to come forward. Constable Perry presented us with plaques for courage and bravery. Next, the attorney general came to the podium and presented each of us with a check for $100,000.00, rewards for each of us who had helped law enforcement put the criminals out of business and behind bars.

Reporters snapped photos of us seven girls and asked some questions. All of us have made appointments for counseling. Beatrice, Sadie, and I are going to see Christina Gonzalez, and the others will be seeing counselors in their areas.

Back on Garden Isle, my head spun with all that had transpired in Augusta. Mama checked the answering machine. There was a message to call Violet Moore.

"Monday night I'd like to invite the twins to be our guests for supper. Please let me know if they can make it. We'll eat at seven o'clock." That was a shocker! Mama rang back that we'd be coming after asking us if we wanted to go.

At the keeper's house other guests included Grand Daddy Moore, Marty, and Lizzy. We dug into a dinner of pork tenderloin, scalloped potatoes, carrots, and blueberry pie. Mr. Moore licked his lips. "Darlin', you've outdone yourself." I looked at Jeanne to see her reaction. *Dear Heaven above, he likes her...* If you think that's difficult to imagine, there's more to be told.

Tears sprang to Violet Moore's eyes. "Can you ever forgive me for my sharp tongue?" She looked at each one of us. "I'm praying that I will remember to think before I speak. Really, I have lashed out at you because I have been so angry with myself. My father was an alcoholic…" She couldn't continue when the shaking sobs made it impossible to talk anymore. Everyone there assured her that she was forgiven.

Otis Moore stood up. "The doc says this old ticker's about run out of steam. I won't be taking Matilda out to sea anymore. If you'll accept her, I bequeath her to you, Marty. I bequeath the squeeze box to Lizzy. God be with each and every one of you. Thanks for the tasty vittles, my daughter. I'd better go home and lay these old bones on my bed." He went to be with Jesus that night, and Daddy preached his first funeral since coming to Garden Isle.

The next afternoon, a Jeep pulled into the driveway. Sebastian and his grandmother got out and came up onto the porch where Mama was shelling some peas for supper. Claire and Sebastian Roberts sat together on the swing grinning from ear-to-ear. "The court awarded me custody this morning." She put her arm around her grandson.

These three last weeks of August ended with Jeanne and me having a heart-to-heart. It happened spontaneously when we womb mates reached out our hands at the same time. Holding both of my hands in hers, Jeanne shared. "I see now that my life belongs to the Lord. I have been selfish and rebellious. Forgive me for being bossy, Ruby."

I answered, "Of course. I already have. Finally, I got it through my thick skull that I'm not the center of attention.

I don't have to always be perfect. In some ways I've been a phony." Holding each other tightly, the Garden Isle twins realized that they had learned lessons that summer that would last a lifetime.

Note From The Author

Dear Reader,

It is my desire to encourage you with the truth that no matter how dire your circumstances, there is hope in God through prayer and people who are willing to be His hand extended. There is no one out of the reach of God's unconditional love. Even though this story is fictional, it reflects how much I know all of this is true.

The setting of an island with mountains and valleys and the ocean with high and low tides is metaphorical of life's experiences. My own life has been one of ups and downs, but I have found His upholding strength. In this story, I sought to show how suddenly one can be lifted high or dropped to a low; no matter which it may be, God's presence is there.

When I wrote that Nathan said, "Maine is like another world," I knew that firsthand, growing up in a small town there. As an adult, I lived and ministered on the coast for many years with my late husband.

I enjoyed writing about the unique Maine oceanic culture of ferries and boats, and seafood. The lingo still brings a smile to my face whenever I hear it spoken. My second husband and I go to the Maine coast once every year. We wouldn't want to miss the squawks of seagulls!

Many experiences I have had with people are highlighted as incidents were brought to mind. Ministry with my first husband began during the Jesus Movement. He went to be with the Lord after we had thirty years of ministry and marriage. We helped and housed people of all ages who were being abused or were in worrisome situations. It was a blessing to witness how Jesus lifted desperate young people out of unhealthy lifestyles.

The Jesus Movement pioneered a relaxed church atmosphere and beloved contemporary worship songs. I incorporated some of my favorites from the 60s and 70s into the story.

My heartfelt prayer for you is that your life will be filled with love, joy, and peace.

www.ingramcontent.com/pod-product-compliance
Lightning Source LLC
LaVergne TN
LVHW011941070526
838202LV00054B/4737